A Wartime Love

#1 International Best Selling Author
Shiralyn J. Lee

ISBN-13: 978-1514715178

ISBN-10: 1514715171

Character Profiles
Stella Baxter
Joan Baxter
Doris Baxter
Harriet Baxter
Mother
Ruth Arnold
Father
Frankie
Bruce
Mrs. Davis, teacher
Mr. Fletcher, headmaster
Clifford Arnold
Mary, factory manager
Sylvia, factory worker
Elsie, factory worker

Artwork and illustrations by Shiralyn J. Lee.

Photo's purchased from Canstock

Copyright: © Copyright at Shiralyn J. Lee July 1st 2015

Copyright @ Shiralyn J. Lee July 1st 2015

All characters within this story are fictional and bear no resemblance to anyone living or dead and are purely coincidental.

A Shiralyn J. Lee story created on July 1st 2015 this book or any parts thereof may not be reproduced in any form, stored in a retrieval system, or transmitted in any form by any means electronic, mechanical, photocopy, recording or otherwise without the prior written permission of the author. Piracy is a crime.

Shiralyn J. Lee stories are downloadable on reputable sites. If for any reason you are reading this for free from a non-reputable site, then you are viewing an illegal download. Please refrain from doing so.

Contact information:

Facebook: Shiralyn J. Lee

Author's notes: I have researched countless blogs, websites, documentaries and movies. I've watched scientific videos on how an explosion affected a 1940s home during the war—seeing the blast in slow motion, for me in the present day, was awe inspiring but for someone who lived through this, I applaud their bravery. This story has been mentally draining for me to write, as it has been set during one of the most horrific times in history. Although I have not physically lived through this war, I do now feel a sense of connection towards it. I was born in England almost twenty-years to the day after D DAY and I grew up with some of the old-fashioned traits that have today since been erased from society. Just the simple task of saving last remnants of soap and then squeezing them together to make a new bar, was thought of as normal back in the 60s but it was something that I had forgotten about, that was until I found a tiny snippet on a blogsite that informed their readers that they did this during the war. We wouldn't think of doing that in this day and age. Sewing the rips in hosiery was another thing that we did, I couldn't imagine anyone walking out with patch up jobs now. I have been living and breathing this story—it has consumed me but I'm glad that it has, as I feel guilty that as someone who has grown up not so long after World War Two, I've forgotten about those who had fought for my country. It was a great reminder that has shown me that a great nation stood their ground and wouldn't show their enemy any weakness.

"How often do you think about your freedom?"

Dedication: For all those who lived, loved and lost during World War II. There were so many lives, young and old, that were taken away. The citizens of the United Kingdom faced their greatest fears and yet with every new dawn, through togetherness, they stood strong and pushed their fears aside. Without the heroes who fought in battles and the heroes who survived the bombings, we would not be where we are today. And for the men and women from countries near and afar, your bravery contributed to keeping a nation great. And for the children, who some were so affected by the travesty of war that they had truly forgotten the art of play.

Acknowledgements: Thank you, ladies, in The Lesbian Book readers Club, for your snippets of information from your personal stories and stories that have been handed down to you by your family members. And to those who sent me links for my research. It is for these people and their bravery that I feel so compelled to write this story.

Thank You: Kev Hammond, for Beta reading.

A special thank you to: Historian Joe Crankshaw. Your knowledge has helped me create an even better visage to my story telling.

Contents

Chapter One	Page 1
Chapter Two	Page 17
Chapter Three	Page 31
Chapter Four	Page 57
Chapter Five	Page 89
Chapter Six	Page 109
Chapter Seven	Page 121
Chapter Eight	Page 141
Chapter Nine	Page 161
Chapter Ten	Page 181
Chapter Eleven	Page 197
Chapter Twelve	Page 209
Fifty Years Later	Page 221

A Wartime Love

Introduction: Set in England, during World War Two, this romantic drama will draw you into the lives of Stella Baxter and Ruth Arnold. The two women meet in an underground station, whilst waiting out an air-raid strike in the early stages of the Blitz over London.

A strong friendship evolves between them—one that eventually turns romantic. But Ruth is a married woman—her husband is overseas, in Germany, fighting for his King and country.

Can a lesbian affair survive not only the tumultuous conditions that an entire nation faces but also, see itself through the fact that Ruth has a husband, willing to die for her freedom?

A Wartime Love

Chapter One

Stella walked along the cobble-stone alley that led to the back yard of her house. She walked slowly—her feet hurt from having just worked a long shift at school—she was a teacher. She taught children between the ages of five-through-to-seven and this was her first position in the working field, she'd only been doing it for a couple of months. She stopped and placed her hand on the brick wall for support and lifted her foot to take off her ankle-strap shoe. She shook it to remove a small stone that had kicked up inside it. Looking over her shoulder to make sure that no one was around, she pulled her skirt a little way up her thigh, revealing the top edge of her stocking. It had slipped down, so she pinched the edging and pulled it back up to prevent the stocking from wrinkling down her leg. She put her shoe back on her foot and carried on walking until she reached the tall wooden green-painted gate at the back of her house. From a middle-class background, she lived with her mother and father and her siblings, Joan, Doris and Harriet, in a three bedroom terraced house in Rodney Street.

A Wartime Love
Shiralyn J. Lee

Her mother had washed the bedsheets. She had secured them with wooden dolly pegs and hung them out on the washing line that had been pushed up high with a piece of two-by-two timber. Stella closed the gate and ran her hand along the white crinkled sheets as she walked past them to get to the house. The brass hinges on the back door that entered directly into the kitchen, squeaked noisily as she opened and closed it.

Her mother, a plump dark-haired woman wearing a lemon-flower-printed dress and a pale-blue wrap-over pinny, was washing the dishes in the kitchen sink. She turned around and smiled at her and then picked up the tea-towel that was hanging from the door knob on the sink cupboard and wiped away the soapy suds from her hands. "Hello, dear," she said warmly. "You're late home this afternoon. Keep you again, did they?" she asked with a silvery voice.

Stella unbuttoned her coat and hung it on one of the hooks on the back door. "Yes, there was an unexpected incident with one of the pupils, I felt so sorry for her. Her mother had gone into labour two weeks earlier than expected and the poor thing had been on her own for most of the day, she just about made it to the hospital after having walked all the way there. I stayed with little Annie until her aunt came to pick her up. Her mother gave birth to a beautiful bouncing baby boy. Oh and she's going to name him Thomas."

A proud and wide smile blossomed across her mother's already cheery face. "Well you certainly are an angel. And where was the woman's husband while all of this was going on?"

"Oh, he had left for work in the early hours. Apparently he works at the docks…Good afternoon, Daddy." She kissed the top of her father's head whilst he sat at the kitchen table reading his newspaper.

A man with greying hair, a grey moustache, and a fattening belly, he ruffled the paper and peered over the top of it. "Oh, good afternoon, Stella."

"Sit down, sweetheart, I'll make you a poached egg on toast and there's plenty of hot tea left in the pot," her mother informed her.

"Oh, thanks, Mum." Stella sat down at the table and removed the crocheted tea-cozy from the tea pot. Her mother handed her a cup and saucer. She placed a tea-strainer over the cup and poured the tea from the pot into it—the steam rose from the cup. "Just what I needed hey, Mum."

"Maybe I should have made a bigger pot," her mother chuckled.

"You say that every day, Mother," her father said from behind his newspaper. "Seems like Germany's not backing down. We could be at war with them fairly soon. Now that won't do at all. It'll affect us all with the economy. We've not even come out of the depression, let alone still feeling the effects of the last war."

"Do you honestly think so, Daddy?" Stella asked him as she blew over her hot tea to cool it.

Her father folded his newspaper and placed it down on the table. "It says it right here in black and white." He pointed to the article in question.

"But what would that mean if we went to war? I mean, would our government send all of our men over there?" she asked her father.

"I should imagine so but I can't see it coming to that," he replied and poured himself another cup of tea. "We're not equipped to go to war. No, this is just a scare tactic, I'm sure."

Stella kicked her shoes off from her feet and wiggled her toes through her stockings—the air—that feeling of relief, brought a welcome smile to her face. "Can I help you with anything, Mum?" she asked as she smelt the toast browning under the grill.

"No, dear, it's practically cooked already." She opened the cupboard door and took out a plate—it had an embossed rim and an old rose pattern in the middle, it was Stella's favourite plate. Her mother buttered the toast and then scooped out the poached egg from the hot water in the saucepan and gently placed it on top of the toast—being careful not to break the yolk.

"Thanks, Mum, you're the best," Stella told her. She always liked to make her mother feel appreciated, as she knew how hard she worked all day slaving over doing the housework, cooking for her and her sisters and her father and making sure that no one went without. She eagerly tucked into her food.

As Stella ate her meal, her sisters Joan, Doris and Harriet, arrived home, closing the front door loudly, as all three of them were deeply engrossed in a conversation about how Joan should change her hairstyle. Joan happened to like the way that her hair looked but her siblings were teasing her and trying to tell her that she should style it differently once in a while.

Joan didn't think much of their teasing and protested vocally—making sure that her voice was being heard over theirs as they entered the kitchen.

"What's all this commotion about?" their father asked. "I'll never get used to having so many women in this house. All day long, it's cackle, cackle, cackle."

"Oh, Daddy, Doris and Harriet are teasing me about changing my hair. I don't want to change it," Joan protested and stomped her foot.

"Well then don't," he answered bluntly.

"What do you think, Stella?" Joan asked her. "Do you think that I should change my hair?"

Stella placed her knife and fork down on her plate. With a smile on her face she looked up at Joan. "I think you should leave your hair just as it is and that Doris and Harriet should stop teasing you about it."

The three of them unbuttoned their coats and hung them on the hook along with Stella's. They sat down at the table, joining their sister and father. Joan removed a small compact mirror from her handbag and then hung it on the back of her chair. She opened the compact up and checked out her rouge lipstick and her hair. Her skin complexion was flawless and had an olive-tone to it, which with her hair being as jet black as it was, gave her an almost modelesque image. She touched the corners of her mouth with the tip of her forefinger to remove some lipstick bleed.

A Wartime Love
Shiralyn J. Lee

Stella pushed her chair back and took her plate to the sink. She dipped it into the soapy suds and using a cloth, she wiped it clean and then put it in the drying rack to allow the sudsy-bubbles to drip down onto the draining board.

"Oh thank you, luv," her mother said. Her chubby apple cheeks glowed as she expressed her gratitude.

Harriet got up and picked three tea cups that were hanging on little brass hooks beneath the wall cabinet and gave one each to Joan and Doris and then one for herself. "I hope there's enough for us all," she said winking as she poured everyone's tea out.

"The high-street was busy today, rather unusual I must say," Doris piped up.

"Well it is half-day closing, so perhaps people were just rushing out to get what they needed at the last minute," Stella answered her.

"Do we always have to talk about shopping? Can I not hear of some intelligent conversations around this table, that's all I ask," their father complained. He had been a butcher all of his life and had retired just over a year ago. He wasn't the sort of man who enjoyed to sit around and do nothing all day, so he had gone and got himself an allotment, where he grew his own vegetables: Runner beans, peas, potatoes, carrots and cabbages. "I'm off to the allotment, Mother," he said getting up from his chair. I'll see you all at suppertime."

"Bye, Daddy," the girls all said in unison.

He gave his wife a kiss on her cheek, went out into the hallway and put on his flat cap and his coat and then walked back through the kitchen, where he left through the back door. They could all hear him whistling as he closed the back gate and walked off down the alley.

"I suppose all of this girl-talk really does put Daddy in an awkward position," Doris giggled.

"Your father does his best, just remember that, girls," their mother told them as she dried the dishes with the tea-towel.

"I bought some lovely fabric to make a dress with. Would you like to see it, Mum?" Joan asked her.

"Oh, and I suppose you want me to make it as well?" her mother asked.

Joan rushed out to the hallway and returned with a brown paper bag. She pulled out the folded rayon fabric. It had an orange background with a small print of pink and white daisies—a colour that really suited her skin-tone. "Isn't it just divine? I do love the colour, don't you, Mum?"

"And do you have any particular style that you want it made into?"

Joan slipped out a dress pattern from the bag. "I bought this too," she smiled fancifully. Her thinly plucked eyebrows arched perfectly over her wide set eyes as she watched her mother examine her fabric choice. "I'll have to check my buttons tin to see if I have any buttons that'll match this material."

"My, you didn't waste any time, did you?" Stella told her sister.

Joan turned her pinched nose up at her sister's comment. "If I'm to find myself a handsome man to settle down with and have two children, a girl and a boy, then I have to look my best now. Heaven's, I'm almost twenty-six, that's considered to be an old maid these days."

Doris got up from her seat and helped herself to a slice of lemon Madeira cake that her mother had made the day before. "This must be one of my favourite cakes in the whole wide world."

Stella reached across the table for her father's newspaper. She looked over at her sister who had devoured a large portion of the slice. "You'd say that about any cake. As long as it's cake, you love it."

Harriet, a baby faced girl, whipped her arm out and snatched the remaining cake from Doris's hand— immediately shovelled it into her mouth with a cheeky grin to go with it.

Doris, her mouth filled with cake, gave Stella and Harriet a mocking smile in return.

•••

It was early-evening. The four sisters sat around the kitchen table podding peas and stringing and cutting the runner beans into horizontal slices. Their father had grown them on his allotment and was very proud of his achievement. They filled a metal strainer with the peas and put the sliced beans into a saucepan of water ready for cooking the next day.

Their father used coal and slack to light the fire in the front room. Once he had managed to catch a flame, he held a sheet of newspaper over the mouth of the grey-tiled fireplace to help draw the flames upward. He could feel the heat behind the paper as it gave off an orange glow and began to roar.

"How's the fire coming along, Daddy?' Stella asked as she walked into the room. She sat down on the olive-green velour settee and crossed her long-slim legs. Her stockings shimmered from the reflection caused by the crackling fire and shadows danced over her unblemished thin-pale face as the flames flickered and drew up the chimney. She pulled out a silk handkerchief from her cardigan sleeve and held it over her narrow nose and blew, causing her luminous pale-green eyes to water up. "Oh dear, I hope I haven't caught a chill."

Her father moved the newspaper away from the hearth and rolled it up into a small ball and tossed it onto the fire. He looked over at his daughter. "Best take some Beechams," he told her.

"I'll be okay, Daddy, I'm just a little tired that's all."

"Well, you mind that you get a good night's sleep," he told her.

"Yes, Daddy, I will."

Doris entered the front room carrying with her a tray with a plate of Huntley and Palmer biscuits and Joan and Harriet brought in mugs of hot milky cocoa. Their mother shortly followed and sat in the chair by the fireplace and removed her slippers and warmed her feet, wiggling her toes.

Their father sat in the armchair on the opposite side of the fireplace and Doris, Harriet and Joan joined Stella on the sofa—all four of them nicely squashed together.

"Well, isn't this cosy," Joan commented.

Harriet was the quieter one of them all. She had a way of being around and yet hardly ever heard. She was the youngest of all the daughters, with Stella being the second youngest and then Doris and then Joan the eldest. Each one of them had their own unique traits. Stella—ash-blonde hair, Joan—almost Cleopatra in appearance, Harriet—baby faced and huge eyes and Doris—short curly hair and blue eyes. None of them looked anything like each other.

Joan passed Stella her mug of cocoa, shaking her hand when she released it, as it had been too hot to hold for any longer. Stella leaned forward and picked out a custard cream biscuit from the plate. She dipped it into her cocoa and then quickly put it in her mouth before it was able to break away.

"Oh, I love custard creams," she said.

"Steady on there," Doris said to her.

"Why don't you turn the wireless on, dear," their mother said to their father.

"All right, Mother, but I don't want any of you chatting away and not letting me hear it," he complained. He got up from his seat and went over to the wireless, where he turned the dial to find the channel.

The news broadcaster was talking about the possibility of war breaking out between Germany and England. There was complete silence in the room as they all listened intently. Once the broadcast had finished they all looked at each other fully concerned.

"It'll be awful if we go to war. I can't even imagine what it would do to this country," Stella said—her eyes darting from one person to another to see if they were all as shocked as she was.

"Nonsense, they're just trying to put the frighteners up us, that's all," Joan said confidently.

"But what if it is true, Daddy?" Harriet asked quietly.

"Joan's right, they are just trying to frighten us. Now, off to bed, all of you," their father told them.

All four girls got up from the settee and gave their parents a kiss before making their way up to their bedrooms. Joan and Doris shared the same room and Stella shared a room with Harriet. Their beds were covered in hand sewn quilted throws, the windows dressed with sheer pink swags and floral drapes, the walls covered in large print pink-flower wallpaper and each girl had their own bed-side table. Stella and Harriet's beds were positioned side-by-side with their headboards on the main wall and then their shared dressing table was on the far wall. An oak wardrobe was placed on the shorter wall by the door.

Stella sat on her bed with her legs crossed. She had dampened her ash-blonde hair and put her rollers in place, securing them with hair pins. Harriet laid in her own bed with the covers pulled up to her neck. She was scared about the possibilities of war breaking out.

Stella smiled sweetly at her—purely for being so innocent. "You'll be all right, Harriet. No one's coming here tonight to disturb the peace."

'How do you know that?" Harriet asked her.

"Because war has not been declared, dear Harriet," Joan called out from her room. "Now get to sleep, both of you before Daddy scorns us all for our disobedience."

"Goodnight, Joan. Goodnight, Doris," Stella said as she pulled back her bedcovers and slipped beneath them. She reached out and switched off the lamp on her bed-side table. The room was dark with just a glimmer of the street light showing through the gap in the curtains.

A Wartime Love
Shiralyn J. Lee

There was very little for them to be afraid of that night.

A Wartime Love
Shiralyn J. Lee

A Wartime Love
Shiralyn J. Lee

Chapter Two

The whistle had been blown at 8.58 a.m. for the children to line up ready to go into their classrooms at precisely 9 a.m. Each class stood quietly in their respective rows in the playground and were then marched inside—led by their teacher.

Stella sat at her desk and behind her she had chalked out three lines across the blackboard and written the letters a b and c on each one. Her pupils were in their first year of school and learning their reading, writing and arithmetic. She was a nice teacher and the children loved her but Mrs. Davis who taught in the classroom across the hallway was a different kettle of fish. Her looks even portrayed her personality with her white-grey hair tied in two plaits and then pinned up on top of her head and her small-rimmed glasses placed on the end of her nose enabling her beady eyes to see. She was mean and extremely stern with the children in her classroom and made use of her wooden ruler when it came to the children's hands. And speaking of hands, each child had the backs and fronts of their hands and their nails inspected before class began and when they returned back from dinner break. Heaven forebode those who had dirt on theirs. It was also the morning for the Nurse to visit and check the children's hair for lice. All of the girls had to have their hair tied up as belief that their hair touching the tables helped in the spread of them.

When the Nurse had finished checking every head, one little girl sat crying at her desk, as she had just been told that she had lice. The other children decided not to sit next to her, which made her feel very alone.

Stella got up from her seat and sat on the edge of the little girl's desk and looked down at her with sympathetic eyes. "It's okay, Amelia. Your mother will make sure to get rid of them and the Nurse will look in on you again this week. Don't be upset, it's happened to a lot of us, even I had them when I was your age. Here, you can write with my special pencil today." She gave her the pencil that she had in her hand and Amelia took it from her. She immediately stopped sobbing and a slight smile crossed her face. She looked over at the other children who were surprised by the gesture made by their teacher. She felt special that day.

Stella slid gracefully off the desk. She walked around the classroom and checked each and every child's hands—fronts and backs and inspected their nails to make sure that they were clean and then strode back to her own desk. She stood in front of her chair. "There will be no more spite in my classroom, have I made myself clear on this matter?"

The children nodded shamefully.

"Good. Now let's begin this class and forget all about any other incidents, shall we." She sat in her chair, tucking her skirt under her legs and shuffled the chair under the desk. "You can copy in your exercise books the first three letters of the alphabet. I shall teach you your ABC's and when you are able to write them with ease, we shall move on to the next three letters in the alphabet."

The children opened up their lined exercise books and copied down what was on the blackboard.

Mrs. Davis's voice was raised and heard by the other pupils in their classrooms. Stella always hated her screech and felt sorry for her pupils, as often, it would be such a trivial reason for her to blow her steam like she did. She got up from her desk and went over to close the door discretely.

A few minutes later there was a knock on her classroom door—it was the headmaster, Mr. Fletcher who peered in through the thick-glass panel. He opened the door and coughed politely to catch Stella's attention that he wanted to talk to her out in the corridor. "Miss.

Baxter, would you mind joining me for a moment?" he asked her.

Stella rose from her chair and told the children to continue on with their work as she left the classroom and closed the door behind her. Mr. Baxter had also called on Mrs. Davis and two other teachers who had classrooms in the same corridor wing.

"This had better be important," Mrs. Davis said, crossing her arms over her chest. Her forehead filled with even more lines and wrinkles, her thin lips turned downwards and showed the bleed lines of her lipstick. "I can't trust those children to be alone for one moment. It's not like their parents are any better than they are, they don't know how to set good examples."

Mr. Fletcher looked gravely concerned—his shoulders dropped, which gave the impression that he wasn't about to give them any good news. "I have just been informed by the local council that we must include air-raid drills for all of the children in this school. They will be sending over the instructions and supplies later on today. It seems as though war will be upon this country soon, I regret to have to say. You will each be responsible for ensuring that the drills are carried out for your class, as requested."

A Wartime Love
Shiralyn J. Lee

Stella held her hand over her stomach as she felt her insides naturally turn over with fear. "How sure are you, Mr. Fletcher?" she asked—her voice trembled and trailed off.

"I fear that there will be a radio broadcast this morning. We're just waiting for Mr. Chamberlain to announce it," he told them. "May God be with us all."

Stella peered through the thick glass in the door to see that her pupils were still behaving themselves, she was assured of their good conduct when she saw that they had their heads down and were writing away.

"Hitler went back on his word for keeping the peace and Germany invaded Poland two days ago. We have no choice but to go to war with them," Mr. Fletcher told them. "I am entrusting each one of you to ensure the children's safety in this school."

Stella's eyes widened. "This is just terrible, Mr. Fletcher."

"It certainly is, Miss. Baxter. We've not even managed to recover from the last war. Let's hope it results in just a battle of words and nothing more."

•••

Word had spread fast across the nation that Mr. Chamberlain would make an announcement from

Downing Street and it would be broadcast at 11.15 a.m. that day. Everyone was on edge.

At 11.15 a.m. precisely, the people of England were informed that their beloved country had officially been declared to be at war with Germany. Mr. Chamberlain announced that the British people would be defending their country for a just cause.

It was almost as if Britain itself had been silenced for those long agonising moments as the words were heard across the country. Shock and fear filled the nation. Many mothers' tears flowed as they knew that their sons and husbands would be taken away from the safety of their loving families. Men—young and old, cheered, as they were eager to join up with the forces and fight for their rights. Some people cheered in the streets, others were speechless and wandered around aimlessly, not knowing what to do. Not one single person was left unaffected.

•••

Stella rushed home to be with her family. She didn't even care that her shoes hurt her feet as she ran over the cobblestones and down through the alley. She opened the back door with force—frantically unbuttoned her coat—her hands trembled as she speedily pushed the buttons through the buttonholes, and then hung it up on the hook and raced to join her family who were in the front room.

Her sisters were seated on the settee, all three of them clutching their handkerchiefs in their hands and crying. Her mother in the armchair with her hand on her chest, patting it gently to comfort herself, and her father, his eyelids almost closed, his pipe rested between his teeth at the side of his mouth, listening intently to the radio broadcasts that were relentlessly being announced.

Stella stepped out of her shoes and left them discarded by the door. She sat on the settee next to Harriet, who happened to have her fingers in her mouth—biting down on them in disbelief at what was being broadcast. Her innocence showed through her tear-filled steel-grey eyes that revealed how much she feared for her safety and the safety of her family. "Say it isn't true, please, Stella, say it isn't," she sobbed.

There were no words of comfort that Stella could offer to assure her sister that war would not come. Instead, all she could do was to put her arm around Harriet and hold her. She softly kissed the side of her face and then rested her head against Harriet's. Joan, who was seated on the far-left seat of the settee, looked across at her two younger sisters. She took hold of Doris's hand, who in turn, took hold of Harriet's—all

A Wartime Love
Shiralyn J. Lee

four of them sat in silence and stared at the fireplace—a framed photograph of their parents' wedding day was placed in the centre of the mantel and surrounded by more photographs of each daughter, and a brass carriage clock to the left that ticked loudly and an ornament of a white cat, placed to the right. The coal and slack glowed a bright-orange with hues of blue—Stella envisioned through the flames, the devastation that war could have—she imagined German planes flying over buildings and dropping bombs and people screaming at the loss of their loved ones. The mere thought of it all caused her to shudder.

"Tea. Perhaps I should make a pot of tea, who wants tea?" Mother asked getting up out of her seat.

"I'll help you, Mum," Stella said and got up to join her in the kitchen. She filled the kettle with water and placed it on the gas stove. Her mum lined up six cups and saucers and put a drop of milk in the bottom of each cup. Stella opened the cutlery drawer and handed her mum a teaspoon. Her mother had a specific order in which she put the sugar into the cups. She always started with her husband's cup, he took three spoons of sugar, then she would have Joan's, then Doris's, then hers, then Harriet's and last in the line-up was Stella's. She always went with the amount of sugar each member of the family took, it was her way of remembering whose was whose.

"I made a jug of barley water for you girls, make sure to drink it tomorrow, won't you," her mother told her.

"Yes, Mum, we will. You do know that you don't have to do that, it's quite easy for us just to open the bottle and pour a tad into a glass and add water to it, it's simply quite easy," Stella informed her.

"I know, dear," her mother said looking over her shoulder. "I just enjoy doing it, that's all."

"Mummy, when you and Daddy married, were you very much in love?"

Her mother, confused, looked over at her. "What an odd question to ask, dear."

Stella leant back against the sink. "I don't think that I can see myself ever getting married. I honestly haven't found anything remotely interesting about any man that I've met…not one."

"Well, dear, I certainly don't find your father to be interesting. In fact, he is quite a boring uneventful man but he does have a good heart, and he takes good care of us all and I do feel that might be more important than someone who is interesting. Interesting doesn't look after what's right in front of them, maybe you need to remember that."

"Perhaps you're right, Mum. It was just a thought that had crossed my mind a while ago."

"Well it all sounds so gloomy, dear. Don't be in such a hurry to meet a boy. When the right one comes along, you'll know about it straight away." The kettle whistle screamed. Mother turned the gas off and using a folded tea-towel, she wrapped it around the handle and picked the kettle up. She poured the hot water into the pot of loose tea—the steam rose up. She gave it a good stir and then placed the lid on the tea-pot.

Stella handed her mother a tray to put the cups and tea-pot on, while she opened the tin of biscuits and picked out one of each choice and arranged them nicely on a tea-plate. "There," she said, happy with her contribution. "That looks lovely, who wouldn't want to devour them all?"

"Don't be too hasty to eat them all, dear, you'll fatten up rather quickly if you do."

"Oh, Mummy, really. Just look at me. I could do with putting on a couple of stone. Sometimes I look at myself in the mirror and wonder why I haven't snapped."

Her mother picked up the tray and then inspected her daughter from head-toe. "I'm sure once you've given me a grandchild or two you'll fill out just fine."

"Oh, Mummy, really."

•••

Joan and Doris sat on Stella's bed, Harriet sat on the woven floor-rug with her legs crossed and Stella sat on the chair at her dressing table. She had a simple collection of items on display, just a glass candlestick, a hairbrush, a crystal glass tray that consisted of Yardley Lavender Water and a lipstick and eyeliner in a glass dish.

They were all dressed in their button-up flannel pyjamas and had their hair pinned in rollers. Joan was reading a story out loud to them all from a book to help take Harriet's mind away from her anxieties. When she finished reading the story, she closed the book and held it close to her chest and with dreamy eyes she looked at the others. "I'm going to marry a handsome man one day. One like Thomas Thornbury," she said, referring to the male character she had just read about in the book.

Doris, her legs crossed and her elbows rested into her knees and her chin propped up by her fisted hands, was preoccupied with pleasant thoughts. "Oh, me too," she said—her eyes filled with a soft glint—her smile subtle, yet suggestive in a way that she could easily kiss the character portrayed in the book. "And what about you, Harriet? Do you have someone in mind that you'd like to marry?" she asked.

A fresh-faced Harriet stretched her legs out and pointed her toes. She gave a moment's thought. "Perhaps. But I don't know if I ever want to leave Mummy and Daddy here all alone in this house. I would hate for them to think that we had all deserted them. Who would Mummy joke with about there being enough tea in the pot? We all know that she says that just for fun."

"Oh what a load of tosh, Harriet," Joan sniped. "Surely you'll want to live in your own house when you marry the man of your dreams? You didn't see Gramps and Nanna living with Mummy and Daddy when they were alive."

Stella reeled her head back. "Hey, what about me? Isn't anyone going to ask me what I want, or don't I count?"

The dimples in Joan's cheeks showed as she giggled. "Oh, dear Stella, you are so sweet but do you honestly care to marry? I've never once heard you speak of finding a man to settle down with. Surely you'll be a spinster until a ripe old age of ninety."

Stella leaned over the back of the chair and picked up a small cushion from her bed and threw it at Joan—hitting her in her shoulder. "You deserve that, you cheeky mare," she joked.

At least it gave Harriet cause to smile.

"All right, time for bed now," Joan told them as she and Doris got up from Stella's bed and headed off out of the room and across the narrow hall to their own room. "Sweet dreams, you two," she said and blew them a kiss from her doorway.

"Sweet dreams," they both replied back.

Once again Stella climbed into bed and turned off her lamp, leaving their room in darkness, apart from the dim glow of the street light.

Harriet snuggled down in her bed and laid on her side with her back facing Stella. She buried the lower-half of her face beneath the bedspread and stared at the shadowy wall. "I know you do that on purpose," she whispered so the others couldn't hear her.

Stella peeked out over the bedcovers. "Do what?" she whispered back.

"Leave the curtain open a slight. I know that you do it for my benefit and I'm very grateful."

"Shush now, Harriet, and get some sleep." Stella turned onto her side and with her hands, palm-to-palm, she placed them on her pillow with her cheek rested on them and closed her eyes.

Chapter Three

October 16th 1939 at 1455 hundred hours, it was reported that enemy aircraft had been sighted just off the coast of Dundee. Ships in the Firth of Forth had been blown out of the water from the bombs dropped by the two German Bomber planes. British Fighter aircraft were deployed to the skies and battled in dogfights against the enemy craft and shot both planes down over the sea, killing the German pilots.

As the people of the nation learned of the attack, a serene calmness embraced once they knew that British fighter planes had taken care of the situation. Instinctively, life continued on as normal.

Every one of all ages had been given gas masks and were to take them everywhere that they went. School children were taught how to carry them correctly and thus giving them the encouragement to show their parents the proper procedure. No one went without and at the beginning of the New Year in 1940 ration books were issued to all family members, buff for all adults, green for pregnant and nursing mothers and children between the ages of five and sixteen, and blue for children under the age of five. Inside the books were small coupons, some were to be torn out of the book and others were for stamping by the chosen shopkeeper.

Barrage balloons had been launched into the air. These were large helium balloons attached to metal cables that were used in hopes that the German aircraft would fly into the cables and crash. There were thousands just floating around…waiting.

Around the country, daylight raids began. Docklands were bombed, aerodromes, and factories. Every home had black-out windows to prevent the enemy from finding the large clusters of houses at night. But on August 24th 1940 the war was set to take on a new direction. Luftwaffe planes had accidentally dropped bombs on London when their target had actually been further to the south—the docks. Many people lost their lives, their loved ones, and their homes. From a city filled with dust and destruction, grew anger and people demanded answers—their blood was on Hitler's hands.

In retaliation to this unfounded attack, Churchill met with the War Cabinet and ordered an immediate strike on Berlin the following day. More than seventy planes were sent to bomb the capital. But Hitler, protesting loudly that the attack on London was not part of his plan, did not see this as a counteracting strike. He saw this as a blatant attack on his homeland and swore revenge on the British.

On Saturday September 7th 1940 the day had been just like any other day in London, as far as normality could be expected. It was a hot day. Many had taken to going shopping in the high street, others were relaxing in the park, riding their bicycles in the streets and children playing games—little girls running with wooden hoops, guiding them with metal rods, boys rolling marbles and swapping them for a range of sizes in their collections and children of all ages chalking the pavement and playing hopscotch.

This day had begun with nothing hinting that anything was about to happen out of the ordinary.

•••

It was Stella's birthday and her mother had made her a small Victoria sponge cake with a light spreading of home-made plum jam and cream that she'd whipped up from a can. She was now in her twenty-fifth year of life.

She sat at the kitchen table with everyone standing around her—her mother holding a flower-patterned china cake-stand with the fresh cake presented on it. They all sang happy birthday to her and cheered to her having another year filled with wonderful things to come.

Harriet held the cake slicer in her hand and was eager to delve into her mother's baking. She nudged Stella playfully. "Shall I slice it for you, Stella?" she asked, anticipating that her sister was going to say yes.

Stella sat back in her seat. Her head turned down, she glanced upwards at her sister, smiled and nodded. She held up her tea-plate ready for Harriet to put her slice on.

At 1643 hundred hours, as everyone tucked into their cake, the air-raid sirens went off. This was not the first time that they had experienced the sirens sounding off, as false alarms had happened previously. But all the same, they had to act as though their lives really were in danger. They had been instructed to not panic and remain calm, and that is exactly what the Baxter family did. They grabbed their coats and gas masks and some rolled up blankets that they had put next to the back door ready to take with them. Stella's mother poured the tea into flasks and Doris hurriedly put the cake into a tin. At this point, they weren't overly concerned.

Their closest air-raid shelter was the underground station which was just moments away and they quickly headed out to it. Many people were walking the streets—all headed in the same direction.

A woman, who constantly looked back over her shoulder, fearing that this might just be the real thing, carried her screaming new-born baby and held tightly onto the hand of her young daughter, who was clearly terrified.

On the pavement, an abandoned musical box. It was open and the ballerina twirled to the classical music.

"We must stick together," Mother, slightly breathless, called out to her daughters.

"We're right behind you, Mum," Joan answered her, encouraging the others to quicken their pace.

Stella smiled at the woman with her baby and daughter. "It'll be all right, you'll see," she said bravely to them.

The woman, her eyes wide, her head low, licked her lips. She tried to break a smile but failed through fear.

As they approached the entrance to Angel underground station, an elderly woman stopped in front of them and looked up to the sky. "What's that noise?" she asked.

A Wartime Love
Shiralyn J. Lee

Stella shaded her eyes with her hand and looked up at the sky. Over the sounds of the sirens, was a vibration like rolling thunder in the distance but the sky was filled with blue and it was cloudless and the full sun shone down on them. Concerned for what it might be, she headed straight for the entrance. "I think we should hurry inside," she told the woman.

Everyone walked down the steep steps in an orderly fashion—echoing footsteps overruled any conversations. An elderly man's walking cane tapped on the tiles as he moved slowly through the crowd. A young boy of seven, or eight-years of age, sneezed. He had no handkerchief, so he wiped the gunky mucus that hung from his nose on the edge of his shirt.

Harriet held Stella's hand tightly. Stella knew that she was nervous, as she could feel how clammy her sister's palm was. She gave a quick reassuring squeeze to comfort her.

When they reached the train platform, they walked along a little ways, past people who had claimed a spot and made themselves as comfortable as possible. Families sat on rugs and blankets, some had flasks of hot tea and cocoa. Stella and her family claimed the next available spot, her mother laid out a picnic blanket on the platform for them all to sit on and even in the silent chaos, she pulled out two flasks containing hot tea from her wicker shopping basket and a tin containing the remainder of Stella's birthday cake. She opened the tin and inside was half a cake and a small silver cake slicer. She divided the cake into small pieces and handed them out to her family. "Well, Stella, at least we will remember this birthday," she said trying to keep them all cheery.

They kept their legs tucked to their sides as people continued to walk past them, many looking exhausted and scared. A woman who was on her own looked at Stella and her family as she approached them. She saw a small gap in between them and the family next to them. "Would you mind if I sat with you," she asked sombrely.

Stella shuffled closer to her family and patted the edge of the blanket for the woman to sit down on. The woman was grateful and quickly sat with them.

"Would you like some of my birthday cake?" Stella asked her. "My mother made it."

The woman's eyes lit up from the sheer kind tone in this stranger's voice. She smiled—her eyelids blinked a couple of times. "Why, that would be very nice," she replied.

"I'm Stella and this is my Mum and Dad, and these are my sisters Joan, Doris and Harriet."

"I'm Ruth, Ruth Arnold. Thank you for the piece of cake, that was very kind of you to offer it."

Stella then held out her small cup of hot tea. "I don't have an extra cup but would you care to share some tea with me?"

Ruth took the cup from Stella's hand and placed her red painted lips to the rim and sipped some of the tea. Her dark eyes gleamed, almost as if they were smiling. "Again, thank you for your kindness," she said handing the cup back. "Oh dear, I seem to have left a lipstick mark, I'm so sorry."

"That's quite all right," Stella assured her.

People still continued to flock to the platform—it was crowded and morale was low.

Low tonal drones coming from up above and vibrations were felt.

A group of men, women and children sauntered by, their clothes were covered in dust, one man had a bandage wrapped around his head and covered one eye. Presumably the woman walking behind him was his wife, she held their new-born baby in her arms—she looked half-scared out of her wits.

Stella's father stood up and touched the wounded man's shoulder—stopping him for a moment. "What's happening up there?" he asked him.

The man, in a slight daze, turned his head to look at her father with his one good eye. His voice was cracked. "They've bombed the East End. Hundreds of Nazi bomber planes are dropping bombs. They looked just like giant Blackbirds flying high in the sky. Many people stood on embankments and watched as the planes grew nearer, myself included. We all saw the bombs drop. We just made it here in time." The man's chin quivered and his head shook as he tried to keep from showing his emotions. "I can't believe that this has happened."

Stella's father compassionately and shook the man's hand. "Rest, my friend, get plenty of rest, you and your family." He sat back down on the blanket next to his wife and placed his hands over his head. He was grateful that they had all taken the sirens seriously and had reached safety before being faced with what was happening outside. He then lifted his head and looked at Stella, Harriet, Doris and Joan. "You will all take these sirens as seriously as we have today. Never under any circumstances think that they might be a false alarm. Do you all understand me?"

He had spoken with fear in his voice—the girls all understood him clearly. Each one of them had widened eyes and stares that were filled with dread.

Stella was surprised by her father's ability to show his emotions in this manner. He had never been the type to display them before. Her mother gently patted her husband's back to comfort him.

"It'll be okay, won't it, Daddy?" Stella, pinching the skin on her thumb nervously, asked him.

Her father rested his elbows on his knees. He had an air of defeat about him as he glanced at his daughters. He tried to speak but words could not leave his mouth. Instead, his disheartened face said it all.

People mumbled amongst themselves as the news travelled through the crowd that London was being attacked and destroyed.

•••

Distant rumbling could be heard coming from above ground. Stella had her arm around Harriet's shoulder and had pulled her in close to make her feel safe. Harriet clenched her fists tight—her fingernails dug hard into the palms of her hands—her eyes were tightly closed, causing wrinkles at the sides. She prayed to herself. Her words were mumbled but Stella could just make them out.

In her apt for showing her braveness, with her sad green eyes, she looked over her shoulder at Ruth.

Ruth placed her hand on Stella's shoulder. "You have a brave assertiveness about you."

"I'm bloody petrified," she mouthed to Ruth so Harriet didn't get wind of it.

Ruth looked up at the curved ceiling as another rumble was heard. She then looked back at Stella. "Me too," she mouthed back.

Stella looked around at the people in her immediate sight. People were still walking past looking for a spot to sit. "Where are your family, did you get caught out somewhere and end up here as the closest shelter to you?"

"No, I live in Duncan Terrace, it's just a few minutes' walk from here.

"So you'll be looking for your family, then?" she asked her.

Ruth toyed with a gold band on her wedding finger. "My husband is overseas right now. He's fighting in the war. We were married the day before he was deployed.

It was an impulsive decision, I don't think that either of us really thought it through."

Stella placed her hand on top of Ruth's and slid it down to her lap. She clasped her fingers in between Ruth's. "I'm sure he's safe," she assured her.

Ruth's gaze moved from Stella's eyes down to their hands, where she studied Stella's comforting behaviour. "He's an RAF pilot," she said, preoccupied with her thoughts.

Stella, distracted by her sister's fear, was unaware that she was stroking Ruth's fingers. "Good for him."

Stella's mother peered over her daughters' heads to get Stella's attention. "Stella. I can't remember if I closed the front door. What if I didn't close it?"

"I closed it, Mummy," Doris answered.

"Oh, good. I'd hate to go home and find that someone had gone inside and taken things."

"I'm sure we needn't worry, Mummy," Joan told her. "People have more important things to worry about right now."

"Yes, you're quite right, dear. It was just a silly thought that popped into my head. I really wasn't thinking properly."

Faint rumblings and vibrations were heard and felt by the people who had found safety in the depth of the underground. Although Stella was good at putting on a brave face, inside, she was crumbling with fear. Each time she felt the light tremors run through her back, as she rested against the tiled wall, she drew in a sharp breath and held it in for as long as she could, keeping her lips closed tightly together to prevent herself from screaming out. Harriet had fallen asleep with her head rested in on her lap and had been spared the ill feeling of dread.

Ruth sat cradling her knees in her arms and held her head low. Her velvety-black eyes were focused on the platform in front of her. "Silence is eerie," she whispered. "You hear more through silence than you bargain for sometimes."

Stella understood what she was saying. With most of the people asleep and those who were awake, listening in silence to sounds of the strikes, it was easy to see what she meant.

•••

The bombing of London continued until at 1810 hundred hours when the all-clear sirens sounded. A sense of elation was in the air as people rose to their feet and gathered their things. They shuffled slowly, one behind the other, making their way to the steep steps and out into the street. The sky-line was different. Orange hues and plumes of white and grey and black smoke rose above the immediate buildings. The smell of burning had drifted in the air. It was so surreal. People coming out of the underground reacted slowly at first—perhaps disbelief and denial protected them from the actual realisation that a portion of their beloved city had just been destroyed.

London docklands were a burning inferno and anyone capable of holding a hose, helped the firemen attempt to put out the fires. But as one building was being concentrated on, another building behind them would catch fire from the sparks being cast in the bellowing black smoke that rose high up into the sky.

No one had time to grieve. They all had a job to do. Finding survivors beneath the rubble and seeing to the dead bodies were their priorities. Loved ones were missing in the chaos, their families not knowing if they were dead, or alive. Young children, alone, screamed in the street, their cries piercing, just wanting their mum's to come and make them feel safe again. Some mother's found their precious babies, others never came.

The Red Cross were run ragged. Their job—to see to the injured—the dead—the unclaimed.

A Wartime Love
Shiralyn J. Lee

The citizens of London had not been defeated, as Hitler had predicted. Their apt for bravery far outweighed the sense of loss in the immediate hours that followed the bombing.

Even normality had been set in place. There were those who continued on with their original plans for the day and went back to shopping in the High Street. One mother told her twelve-year old son to go home and that she would see him there in a couple of hours, ready to cook his tea. She gave him a kiss on his cheek and waved him off as he ran back to wherever it was he had been playing earlier.

The assumption of safety had been set in place.

Stella followed her family out from the underground. They too, were taken by the colour of the sky and the burning smells that drifted.

Ruth stood close to Stella. They looked at one another, their eyes—something in their eyes—in their gaze—something made them understand that they would be seeing each other again.

Ruth brushed a few strands of her dark-hair back behind her ear, revealing her thin face and structured cheekbones. She held out her small hand for Stella to shake. "You have been so kind to me and thank you for that lovely piece of cake, it was very generous of you to share it."

"It was my pleasure, I'd do it again if I had to," Stella replied.

Ruth radiated with a look of hope. "We'll meet again, I'm sure of it."

Stella nodded and then joined her family on their walk home, looking back over her shoulder intermittently at Ruth until she was out of her sight.

Just on the short walk home, the Baxter's came across a group of teenage boys headed for the docklands to help put out the fires. There was also a little girl with ribbons in her hair, wearing a lemon satin dress and ankle socks, skipping with a rope in her front garden, and a middle-aged housewife on her knees, scrubbing her doorstep clean, and an elderly gentleman wearing a flat cap, standing at his garden gate, smoking a pipe—he nodded at them as they walked past him.

Stella was confused by the ordinariness. She couldn't understand how these people could carry on as if nothing had just happened to them but in one sense, nothing had actually happened to them…yet.

•••

A Wartime Love
Shiralyn J. Lee

They arrived at their front garden gate. Their home, along with everyone else's had been unaffected by the chaos. The street pavement was lined with young sycamore trees—their leaves dark green and leathery and their seeds looked like angel wings when they would fall and be caught by the wind that would take them away. Stella felt a sigh of relief at seeing the familiarity of her home and its surroundings.

"I'll make us all a lovely cup of tea," her mother said as she opened the green-painted four-foot high gate.

They congregated around the kitchen table—picking up where they had left off earlier. They sang happy birthday to Stella and then handed her a present. It was wrapped in Christmas paper that her mother had saved from the previous Christmas holiday. She carefully opened it, knowing that her mother would save the paper for another celebratory present. It was a bar of Pears soap, Stella's favourite. Also a dress that her mother had handmade, it had a small-flower print and a plain neck-line. Stella loved it.

"We put our ration coupons towards the fabric, me, Harriet and Mum," Doris said.

"I have something for you too," Joan said, handing over a small flat gift wrapped in newspaper and tied with brown garden string.

A Wartime Love
Shiralyn J. Lee

"Oh, what could this be?" Stella asked, opening it. She pulled out a bar of chocolate. "Joan, where on earth did you get this?"

Joan, with her hands clasped behind her back and a huge grin on her face, swayed happily. "I've met someone and he's a soldier."

Stella looked up at her from her seat. "What? You didn't say anything."

"I wanted to be sure about him first. He's in the army and his name is William but all his chums call him Will. He also looks quite dapper in his uniform."

"Joan, you'll mind your manners in this house. And if you're as serious as you sound about this William boy, then perhaps you should practice the good manners that you've been brought up with and kindly bring him round to meet your parents," her mother told her.

"Just as soon as he has his next free day, I will, Mum, I promise."

"Right. Let's get some tea on, girls, before we all starve to death," their mother told them.

She opted for some cold ham and slices of tomatoes that her husband had grown on the allotment and carved a few slices of bread from the loaf she had made the day before. Everyone sat around the table and ate.

"I need the loo," Doris announced to everyone. "I think all that tea has gone right through me."

"Better hurry, then. I need to go too," Joan told her.

Doris raced upstairs to the bathroom and closed the door hard behind her. The bathroom consisted of an enamelled cast iron bath with a line drawn all around it marking five inches for the water ration. The window, framed with pink-swag curtains, had tub of dad's shaving cream, shaving brush, a cup with toothbrushes and a container of talcum powder on the sill. On a wooden chair at the end of the bath, was a wooden box with a first aid kit inside. The toilet cistern was attached high up on the wall above the toilet with a long pull-chain hanging down from the side of it to flush the toilet with. They were part of the elite at having an indoor toilet, as this was still uncommon in most houses.

•••

As darkness fell over the Capital city, a second attack loomed and at 2010 hundred hours the air-raid sirens sounded again. This time everyone took the warning more seriously.

A Wartime Love
Shiralyn J. Lee

Stella's mother grabbed hold of her shopping basket that had been filled with food items from the cold-larder. Tomatoes, bread and a small piece of cheese. She had recently boiled some water in a saucepan and made two flasks of cocoa, so Stella grabbed them to take. The family then left the house and hurried to the safety of the underground once again. But this time the gates were closed and padlocked. Tempers rose as citizens needed shelter immediately. They could feel tremors beneath their feet as bombs dropped over houses in the near distance and the boom sounds grew closer. A few of the men became angered at the closure of the gates and together formed a team to break the gates free from the walls. They succeeded and the people rushed inside, down the steep steps and on to the platform—some even picked the same spot where they had taken just a few hours earlier.

This time they could feel the domed walls of the underground vibrate against their backs as the bombs dropped closer and the anti-aircraft guns fired up into the darkening skies at the enemy planes. The homes being bombed could have been anyone of theirs—now the war was actually happening to them—now they feared for their lives, their families and their homes.

The Baxter's sat on their picnic rug and settled down amongst the many. Stella looked around to see if she could catch sight of Ruth anywhere. She pursed her lips and shook her head in frustration because people were constantly walking in front of her view. Not content with the situation, she stood up and stretched up on her tip-toes, peering as best she could over the oncoming crowd.

Her wish was answered when she saw Ruth making her way along the platform. "Ruth, Ruth," she called out to her, waving her hand frantically.

Her mother and father looked up at her, wondering why she was yelling out so excitedly.

Ruth pushed her way through the crowd, she was happy to see a friendly face. Not understanding whether it was a justified feeling of dread, or a moment of relief but as soon as she was close enough, she threw her arms around Stella and hugged her tightly. Stella responded to the hug. Both women felt a draw towards each other—neither one of them understood what it was.

As the evening went on, so did the incessant falling of bombs and although they were in a safe place, they could still hear faint booms and crumps and vibrations, possibly caused by buildings being blown to pieces.

Two women walked by holding trays with cups of cocoa and offered them out to anyone who was in need of one. The Baxter's, along with others, ate their tidbits. Ruth had brought a packet of biscuits and a flask of tea. She shared her snacks, as the Baxter's shared their food with her.

The bombing of London continued throughout the night. Thousands of bombs had destroyed medieval buildings—churches that Christopher Wren had re-built after the Great Fire of London, had burnt to the ground. The constant destruction had affected the greater portion of city.

There were many people who had chosen to stay in their homes and wait out the raid—some hiding in the cupboard beneath their staircases—others huddled under dining tables in their front rooms and then there were those who had chosen to erect their own bomb shelters in their back gardens, known as Anderson shelters, made from curved galvanised steel panels.

People in the underground had settled down for the night and slept as best they could, some remained awake and played card games, and others read a book while holding a gas lamp to read. With everyone being in such close proximity, odours drifted. Body odour gave off a pungent smell, alcohol emitted from the skin of those who drank and smokers lit up their cigarettes and smoked at leisure.

A Wartime Love
Shiralyn J. Lee

At 430 hundred hours the all clear sirens sounded. People were woken up and again, gathered their belongings before making their way out into the open. They did not expect the devastation that faced them. Their London, the city that they had grown up in, the city that they had shopped in the day before, had been re-mapped forever.

The smell of gasoline from the bomber planes lingered in the air—black smoke and drifting soot filled people's nostrils. The horizon of the city was lined with the colour orange—thick dust loomed overhead. People held handkerchiefs over their mouths to enable themselves to breathe. Shards of glass crunched underfoot as people walked aimlessly over debris that coated the streets.

A poster on a shop window that was surprisingly still intact read, 'Don't wave your torch to catch the bus. Use a white cloth to flag it down.'

A double decker bus, with minor damage to it, had passengers still in their seats, each one looked as though they were waiting but on closer inspection they were all dead. Not a scratch, or any sign of injury had been laid upon them. It was as though they were sleeping. The pressure of the glass being sucked out had also sucked their lungs out instantly.

A Wartime Love
Shiralyn J. Lee

Half-blown out houses looked like dolls houses. Pitting on the brickwork had been caused by flying shrapnel and a tram had been blown onto its side and into a building.

Stella's stomach flipped over when she saw the devastation before her. Her parents gathered her and her sisters' close. "We must be brave and expect the worst," their father said to them.

Ruth very lightly stroked Stella's arm to gain her attention. "I must be going. I'm dreading finding my home in ruins, I just don't know what I'll do if it's gone." Her eyes filled with sadness.

"Mummy, Daddy, I'm going to go with Ruth to make sure that she's all right," Stella, feeling independent, told them.

Her parents and her sisters looked horrified at her for even suggesting that she was going elsewhere at such a dire time. "Surely not, Stella," her father protested.

"Daddy, I'll be fine. I think Ruth needs someone to be with her. How would any of you feel if you were on your own having to face the unknown?"

Ruth shook her head at Stella. "No it's okay. I'll be fine, honestly."

A Wartime Love
Shiralyn J. Lee

"No you won't," Stella retorted. "I'm sure that my family would completely understand if the shoe was to be put on the other foot." She looked at them all sternly. "Well?"

"All right, all right," her father agreed. "But make sure that you are home within the hour...that is if we still have a home."

'Thank you, Daddy. I promise that I'll be home soon." She kissed his cheek and then her mother's.

"Don't be long, Stella," Joan told her.

Harriet looked timid and scared. "Darling, Harriet, please don't fret. I promise that I will be home shortly."

"I'll wait on the doorstep for you," she answered in a mouse-like voice.

Stella kissed her cheek. She put her hand in her pocket and pulled out her silk handkerchief. "Swap hankies with me," she told Harriet.

Harriet searched her coat pocket for her own handkerchief. She handed it over to Stella and Stella gave her hers. "I remember when we used to do this when we were little," she told Stella.

"It means I'm coming home, darling Harriet." She shoved Harriet's hanky inside her coat pocket and then headed off with Ruth.

Chapter Four

It wasn't too far to walk to Ruth's house in Duncan Terrace. Many houses had been blasted to the ground. Piles of rubble spread across every inch of what used to be a road and the thick dust had settled. The oddity and eeriness of seeing one house left standing unscathed by the bombings and its neighbour completely destroyed to a pile of nothing was very hard to take in. Ruth, along with so many others, had no idea what to expect when she reached home.

They turned the corner into Duncan Terrace. Ruth stopped. She took hold of Stella's hand and closed her eyes. "I can't bear to look. I know that's so selfish of me but I just can't."

Stella looked at the houses in the Terrace. Most of them had been untouched and the one's that had been touched had suffered just minor damage with broken windows and a garden gate or two that had been broken from their hinges. "It's quite all right, I think you'll find that you can look."

Ruth opened her eyes and quickly inspected the houses in the Terrace. She looked behind them at the devastation and destruction and then back to the few houses in her little secluded part of the neighbourhood. She placed her hand over her mouth and still holding Stella's hand, she led the way to her two bedroom home. They stood at the front gate. There wasn't much in the way of a front garden, just a small patio area where a lavender bush and some pansies had been planted beneath the small bay window. Ruth nervously fumbled around in her coat pocket for the door key. "I'm sorry, I seem to be struggling with nerves trying to get this key out of my pocket."

"There's no need to apologise, Ruth. I quite understand. At least we can see that this area didn't take a bashing from Hitler."

Ruth let out a sigh of relief. "Yes. He didn't get us all." She put the key into the lock and turned it. The green painted door with a circular piece of decorated glass on the top half, opened. Ruth stepped inside first.

Stella followed her in and closed the door behind them. It was a very similar design to her own home but on a smaller scale. The stairs on the right, faced her and then a narrow hallway with a patterned runner rug on the floor. A door on the left and a door at the end of the hallway. Ruth opened the door on the left that led into the front room. It was very quaint. The fireplace was surrounded by wooden panelling and turquoise tiles decorated around the mouth of the fire. A round clock on a dark-wood base, ticking away, was the only item that decorated the mantel. The floral curtains were delicate and drawn closed to hide the ugly brown paper on the window pane. A table next to the fireplace had a radio on it and next to that was a writing bureau with tall cabinet on top of it that had glass doors and quaint little ornaments on show. There was a biscuit-coloured two-seater settee and a matching armchair, both with a cream linen cloth over the backs of them.

Watercolour paintings decorated the walls. Stella inspected them. "Oh, I like this one. Where is this?"

"It's a painting of Ramsgate seafront. I painted it when I was there a few years ago."

"You painted it? It's very good."

"It's all untouched," Ruth said quietly, as she looked around the room.

Stella joined in looking around the room and was drawn to a photograph on a side-table next to the settee. It was a wedding photo of Ruth and her husband. He was in his RAF uniform and she was wearing a lace dress and matching veil. "This is your husband?" she asked her.

A Wartime Love
Shiralyn J. Lee

Ruth turned around to see Stella holding the framed picture. She nodded her head. "Yes. Clifford, that's his name in case you were wondering."

Stella examined the photograph more. She wasn't looking at the handsome man in it, her eyes were drawn to the solemn face of her new found friend. "You look sad."

Ruth walked over and stood slightly behind her—her shoulder brushing up against Stella's. She looked at her picture, studying it for a moment. "I never quite saw it as that before," she said. "But you're quite right, I do look rather sad."

Stella placed the picture back in the same spot that she had removed it from. "Well I can imagine that this room gets a lot of sun during the daytime."

"Yes, it used to, before I had to blackout the windows. I'm sure it will again soon, no doubt."

Stella flapped her hands at her sides. "Well, I can see that you're all right here. I best be getting home before my family wonder where I've got to. They do tend to worry, especially now and especially Harriet. She's the youngest in our family and the dear is simply a darling. Oh, gosh, listen to me just rambling on. Well, I really must go now."

"Please let me see you to the door," Ruth offered, with her hand out to shake.

Stella extended her hand and shook Ruth's. "Thank you," she replied.

They walked out of the front room with Ruth following closely behind Stella.

Stella opened the door and stepped out. She turned around to shake Ruth's hand again.

"Perhaps we can visit properly one day?" Ruth asked her as she shook her hand.

Stella beamed with delight. "Yes. That would be rather lovely. Let's hope that this is the end of the bombing and we can all get back to living normal lives once again." She turned and waved as she closed the small gate.

Ruth rested the side of her face against the open door—her eyes pursued Stella as she walked away. Once Stella was out of sight, she sighed heavily and closed the door…

•••

Debris and devastation lined the streets. Stella had no choice but to make her way through it.

A Wartime Love
Shiralyn J. Lee

A group of people, covered thickly in dust, were down on their knees frantically removing broken bricks, pieces of furniture and twisted steel girders. One of the women was distraught—crying out—almost grievingly, "Save my Edward! Oh please, dear lord, save my little boy." Blood trickled over her hands, merging with the grey powder that coated her skin, as she desperately dug through the mess.

A low tonal murmur was heard beneath the rubble.

"Shush!" a man quickly told them. He listened with his head turned and his hand cupping his ear. "I can hear him. He's alive. Your little boy is alive," he cried.

The group of people dug faster, knowing that time was of the essence. Stella dropped to her knees and joined in the rescue. They had to act fast but maintain the upmost caution in order not to disturb anything that would cause harm to the boy.

After several minutes, they had managed to free a small, very frightened, boy. Thankfully he was still alive. His clothes were torn and filthy, he had cuts and grazes over his face, arms and legs. One of the men scooped him up in his arms and with the boy's mother, ran down the street to take him to safety—if that's what you could call it.

Stella stood up. Her dark-grey wool coat was filthy and her hands and face covered in black smudges from the charred remains. She drew in a deep breath and exhaled it slowly.

Arriving at her front garden gate, she was greeted by one very happy Harriet, who had been sat on the doorstep waiting for her safe return. Harriet jumped to her feet and raced to the gate to meet her. "Stella, I was so worried about you. If any more planes would have attacked, I think I would have surely died, I simply would have." She threw her arms around her sister and hugged her.

"Please don't worry about me. I was perfectly safe and besides, did any sirens sound off? You must learn to be brave, dear Harriet, I'm not always going to be around."

They went inside the house and joined the others.

Stella's mother was busy. She had boiled water in saucepans and made flasks of tea in case of another attack. She had also sliced up the remains of the cold ham and wrapped them and placed that inside her wicker basket in the cold larder and prepared some raw carrots and wrapped some home-made jam tarts. "There! That'll show that Hitler. At least we'll have a picnic fit for a king," she boasted, wiping her hands on the skirt-part of her pinny.

Joan and Doris were up in their bedroom. Joan had put her lipstick in her pocket and also a small compact mirror.

"Why on earth do you need that?" Doris asked her.

"Darling, Doris. Surely you don't expect a practically engaged woman to leave her home looking as though she's just got out of bed. If we have to leave here in a hurry again, I'm going to be prepared."

"So you're telling me that you'll defeat Hitler with a smidgen of lipstick? And what's with the practically engaged announcement?" Doris asked her.

"Engaged? Who's engaged?" Stella asked—a smile broadening and her eyes lighting up as she peered in through their bedroom door.

Joan was seated at her dressing table, admiring her appealing reflection in the mounted mirror—her eyes roamed over the mirrored glass to look at Stella. "I said practically engaged, if you really must know. Anyway, at least one of the Baxter girls should make some sort of effort to marry off soon and produce a child or two. I'm sure that Mummy and Daddy are just itching to be grandparents."

A Wartime Love
Shiralyn J. Lee

Stella leaned against the doorframe. She wasn't so sure about her sister's opinions. "Even in a time of war and uncertainty you think that it would be a good idea to marry and create new life?"

Joan raised an eyebrow and twisted her mouth to one side. She turned around on her seat to face Stella and placed her hands on the back rest and looked her sister directly in her eyes. "I will never allow anything to stop me from being a wife and a mother. I'm sure that if you had any maternal feelings inside of you, you would understand what I was talking about. Sometimes, Stella, I do have to worry about you."

"I didn't mean any harm by my thoughts. I was just thinking about how hard it's been over the past year. Simple things that we've always taken for granted have been taken away from us. A child wouldn't even know what natural daylight coming into a house is like. Look at us, Joan. We have to have lights on in the middle of the day. I was just trying to point that out, that's all."

Joan shifted back to face her reflection in the mirror. Her eyes were narrowed and produced tiny lines at the sides and her mouth shut tightly, causing dimples to show in her cheeks. "Now you've made me look like a horrid witch. Really, Stella, I do wish you'd be more considerate when a woman such as myself, is trying to make herself presentable in a most fashionable way."

Doris, on her side with her elbow propping her up, had been reading a book on her bed. She lowered it and raised her eyes over the top of the pages to look at Stella. "Not everyone can live according to Hitler's plans, you know. Life still has to go on."

"I know it does, Doris. That's not what I'm trying to say here. I just worry over the children being brought into a world where war seems to dominate."

"Well, I think you should worry more over how you look. What on earth happened to you?" Joan asked her.

"I just helped to rescue a small boy from a pile of rubble. His mother was just so distraught over the thought of losing him." Her eyes turned watery. She wiped beneath her eye when a tear trickled out and down the middle of her cheek, creating a clean-stain-line through the black. "I must look terrible."

"Oh, dear Stella, we didn't mean to make you cry." Joan said, as she got up from her chair and gave her sister a heart-felt hug.

"It's not that. I'm tired. I'm so tired," she sobbed.

"Oh poor, Stella," Doris said and got up to join her sisters in a loving hug.

•••

A Wartime Love
Shiralyn J. Lee

Again that night, another bomb raid came. They went to the same underground and sat more or less in the same spot. Ruth joined them and with the power of their British spirit, they kept themselves busy with conversations, knitting, and card games and sleeping.

Stella and Ruth were able to share small snippets of information about their lives with each other. It seemed strange that they could chat away and be oblivious to the ongoing influx of people trudging past them, feeling tired and looking overcome with fear. They sipped on hot tea and shared slices of ham, jam tarts and some biscuits that Ruth had brought with her. In a strange way it made the two women feel almost comfortable being on the train platform whilst the bombing took place up above.

Ruth came to know that Stella still lived in the same house that she was born in and that she had never had any actual interest in boys. Stella found out that Ruth had spent her childhood growing up in White Oaks, South London and had met her husband through a mutual friend. Her parents had her in their later years of marriage and both had passed away by the time she had reached her twenty-first year of life. She had inherited a nice sum of money from them, as they had been pretty well off. This money had paid for the house that she and her husband now owned. Stella also found out that the women in Ruth's family had a history of losing their unborn babies before their third month and that Ruth was too scared to even contemplate having children.

•••

There had been consistent nights of bombing from German planes over the city of London and now they had experienced more than twenty nights of strikes. Not just houses had been demolished but in some cases, entire streets had been destroyed. Nothing but piles of broken bricks, burnt roof beams and scattered personal possessions, lay across what used to be the streets that people walked down and vehicles drove on. People had worked together and made clearings for access. The firemen, exhausted, had fought hard to put out the fires day and night.

Churchill had paid a visit to see the devastation for himself. He announced that every man, woman and child were doing well in the face of evil. But morale with the people was wearing thin at this point.

Radio broadcasters interviewed people affected by the bombing. They compared their similarities when being asked the question:

'What do you want Churchill to do about it?'

A Wartime Love
Shiralyn J. Lee

The responses came in many words but all meaning the same thing.

> 'Ruddy-well give the Germans back what they deserve.'

•••

Stella's father had returned from his allotment. After so many bombings, it had finally fallen victim to destruction. There was nothing left that even remotely looked like an allotment. Although her father was saddened by this loss, he knew that he couldn't compare it to the loss of life and homes that a lot of his friends and neighbours had suffered. He thought himself lucky that so far during these raids, their home had been saved from being bombed.

•••

The Baxter's had made their way to the underground and settled in their spot before the sirens had sounded. They had even made friends with a few of the people who had settled on spots close to them over the past few weeks.

Stella sat on the picnic rug and waited for her friend to turn up. An hour past by and still she hadn't shown herself. Stella became agitated at not knowing where she was.

A Wartime Love
Shiralyn J. Lee

She sat with her nails in her mouth, biting them nervously. Her mother tapped her on her hand and wagged her finger at her for the bad habit. But Stella couldn't concentrate. Her thoughts were for the worst and all she could think, was that Ruth could possibly be dead.

She looked at her mother—her eyes filled with tears and despair. "Is this what it does?" she asked her—her chin trembling.

Her mother—her eyes filled with hurt for her daughter and the people around her, brushed the back of her hand over Stella's flushed cheek. "I'm sure your friend must have been caught out somewhere. Maybe she was out shopping with a friend and has taken shelter elsewhere." She gave her an assuring smile.

Stella wasn't used to not having an answer for her own dilemmas. She couldn't face thinking about what might have happened to her friend, because if she did, then that would mean all sorts of horrid emotions she would have to cope with. The one thing that she had managed to do throughout this war so far, was keep the reality at bay. This had given her the strength to be who she was and to cope with the everyday things that were being cast upon her and her family, and the people surrounding her. The unknowing was the absolute worst for her. It played games with her mind—ideas that Ruth may be badly hurt, or even dead—her body just sprawled over rubble with no family to claim her. Stella shuddered and then gave out a whimper.

Harriet took hold of her hand and squeezed it tight. "Dear, Stella, please don't despair."

Stella placed her arm around her sister and trembling, she hugged her. "As soon as the all clear is given, I'm going to Ruth's house to see if she's all right. She lives in Duncan Terrace. If I fail to return home you'll know to look for the dark-green front door with a lavender bush planted close by. Please remember that, Harriet," she whispered in her ear.

Harriet, her head tilted, her long wavy strawberry-blonde hair covering her youthful rosy cheeks, reeled back. "But you can't go, Mummy and Daddy won't let you, I'm sure of it."

"Nothing will stop me. If there is another strike and I don't make it here on time, you'll know where to find me." She kissed her sister's head and then tugged the woollen blanket up over her shoulders. They snuggled together and fell asleep to the faint crumps and booms and vibrations that they had become accustomed to.

Hours had passed and the dawn skies were spreading over the nation. The all clear sirens sounded and once again the public went about life as best they could—

each day getting a little harder to swallow, as the death toll grew larger and the levelled homes became more apparent.

Stella and her family emerged from the dark underground. There was no dawn sky for them, instead, they looked up to the same disturbing hues as they had done for the past few weeks. The oranges and greys and whites of fire, smoke and dust, were the reminders of what had been lost during the night—a sight that they wished to be in their past.

Stella, standing directly behind Harriet, took hold of her arm and held her back from the others. "Not a word, Harriet. Not unless you desperately have to, do you understand?" she told her sister in confidence.

Harriet nodded. She lowered her head and glanced secretively through her hair at her parents and other two sisters. "Duncan Terrace, dark-green door," she whispered.

"Every time that we leave here I tend to wonder whether we still have a home to go back to," their father said to them.

Stella looked to her parents. "Mummy, Daddy, I have to be somewhere, please don't worry, I'll be quite all right."

A Wartime Love
Shiralyn J. Lee

Joan cocked her head and scrunched up her nose. "But where on earth could you need to be? Surely it's more important for you to find out if we still have a home to live in?"

Stella, unyielding, prised herself away from her family and took a few steps back. "Go on ahead without me, I'll be fine. You have nothing to worry about, I promise." Before they could argue with her, she had already quick marched it down to the corner of the street. She looked back and waved at them to carry on home. She was determined to find out what had happened to her new-found friend.

...

Stella couldn't deny the fact that the onset of panic had riddled its way through her mind. She hurried—passing wandering crowds of people who were eagerly searching for their loved ones after being separated from them during the night.

A whole house had been levelled—its neighbours on both sides had had their walls ripped away, showing their internal rooms destroyed and blackened with soot, and portions of walls revealing the patterned wallpapers. A milk bottle—still sealed and undisturbed on the doorstep of a bombed house, where it had been delivered the afternoon before. The sun shone down on

A Wartime Love
Shiralyn J. Lee

blackened structures through pockets of drifting smoke and dust. Craters in the middle of streets—gas pipes and water mains broken. A double-decker bus had been slammed into a building, the only part visible was the advertisement, 'Coughs and Sneezes Spread Diseases,' on the back beneath the upper-deck window. Steel girders that once supported magnificent buildings, jutted up out of the ground. A church bell that once rang from a tall steeple, lay on top of twisted pipes—the church was now just a pile of rubble. And luscious green trees that had once lined the pavements, with leaves that rustled in the warm summer breeze, had been reduced to nothing more than large dead-looking twigs sticking out of the dirt.

Disturbing thoughts filled Stella's mind, as she fretted for her friend's life.

"Oh, Miss. Have you seen a small boy? I can't find him. He was playing around this area a short while ago and now I can't seem to find him. He was wearing a cap and a blazer and grey shorts," a woman on the other side of the street called out to her.

Stella stopped abruptly. She glanced around her immediate surroundings to see if there was a small boy of that description. "No, I haven't. I'm so sorry. If I do see him, I shall report it to the first policeman that I come across," she told her sympathetically.

She carried on and turned into Duncan Terrace, where she was thankful to see that none of the buildings had been harmed. She opened the gate and rushed to Ruth's front door—wrapping her knuckles loudly on the green paint. Ruth didn't answer. Stella—on the doorstep, listened for any sounds of footsteps approaching. Perturbed, she lifted the brass knocker tapped that, again, no answer. She stepped back and looked up at the bedroom window and then across to her right at the front room window. She reached over and tapped the glass pane. "Please be all right Ruth, please be here," she said to herself. When no answer came, she opened the letterbox and peered in. Her eyes widened in disbelief at what was before her. "Ruth!" she cried, when she saw her lain face down on the floor at the foot of the stairs. Ruth didn't move. "Ruth, Ruth, it's me, Stella, I'm going to try and get in." She pulled her hand from the letterbox and desperately tried to find a way to gain entrance.

Ruth's house was the third one in a row of six and to the left of her portion was an arch-shaped walk-through that gave access to get to the backs of the houses. Stella ran through it and around to Ruth's back door. She tried the handle and found that the door wasn't locked. She opened it and went inside. "Ruth," she called to her, as she dropped to her knees at the side of Ruth's unconscious body. Placing her hands carefully on

Ruth's shoulders, she turned her over. A gash ran across her forehead. "Oh, Ruth, please don't be dead." Tears filled Stella's eyes and in the blurriness of her vision she caught site of red marks on the white-painted wooden stairs. On further inspection, she noticed that Ruth's skirt was wet. She lifted the hem and saw dried blood on both of her inner thighs. "Oh, no."

There was no time for Stella to think. She got up fast and opened the front door. Looking quickly, she caught a neighbour's attention and cried out to her.

An older woman, who was sweeping her front path, stopped when she heard a cry for help. She dropped the broom and paced quickly, where she followed Stella inside Ruth's house. She didn't take long to conclude what had happened. "Better get her into the front room and lay her down on the settee. I doubt whether the doctor will be able to come and see to her though, not with all what's going on, so we'll just have to make do as best we can. Were you with her when she lost her baby?"

Stella, kneeling over Ruth and stroking her hair, looked at the woman confused. "Baby?"

"She was with child. Now, we need to get her in the front room and cleaned up and once she's comfortable, I'll send my Archie down to the hospital to inform my niece. She's a nurse, you know, and a good one. She gets on with the job in hand. My name's Mable, by the way and my niece is Rosie."

They lifted Ruth, carefully supporting her, as they carried her into the front room. Mable went into the kitchen and put a saucepan of water on to boil. Stella stayed with Ruth, holding her limp hand in hers and stroking the back of it. Once the water was ready, Mable poured it into a bowl with a little cold water and picked up a tea-towel—throwing it over her shoulder. She hand washed Ruth's legs, gently wiping away the dried stains.

Stella, using a scrubbing brush and a pale of water, vigorously scrubbed the red marks from the stairs.

"Better fetch her some clean clothes. These'll need to be washed," Mable called to her from the front room.

Stella stopped scrubbing. She wiped her hands dry on the pinny that she had taken from the kitchen to protect her clothes. "Okay," she said wearily. She made her way upstairs, where three closed doors faced her. She opened the first one—it was the bathroom—a small one with green tiles and white lace covering the blackened window. Stella closed the door. She turned around and opened the next door. It was Ruth's bedroom. She entered gingerly. The room was simplistic—a dark solid-wood wardrobe with a mirrored door and four drawers, a small chest of drawers with a man's hairbrush and a notebook on top, presumably her husband's. A kidney-shaped dressing table with a three-way mirror and a pair of stockings hanging over. A black ebony hand-held mirror, a glass tray, hairbrush and some makeup items were all neatly placed. She paid particular attention to the bed and ran her fingers along the black spindly metal frame. This was where her friend had laid with her husband and made love to him and conceived her baby. She moved around to the side of it and just for a quick moment she sat down on the cream linen bedspread. The mattress was firm. There was a side table with a small cream-shaded lamp, a silver-framed photograph of her husband and a brass carriage clock. "Oh get a grip on yourself," she muttered. Snapping out of her stupor, she went to the wardrobe and opened the door. There were some men's clothes hanging neatly over some wooden hangers and pushed to the left. Ruth's clothes hung on the right side. Stella picked out a cream satin blouse and a grey skirt. She also opened the top drawer in the chest and picked out some undergarments. She closed the drawer slowly, looked around the room again and then left, closing the door softly behind her.

She and Mable undressed Ruth and then changed her into fresh clothes—all the while, Ruth remained in a dormant state.

"She'll need plenty of rest for the time being, and she won't be fit enough to make it down to the shelter for a night or two, I'm sure of that. Your best bet is to make a safe place under the stairs for her to shelter during the raids," Mable told her.

Stella fiddled nervously with her fingers and nodded in agreement. "Well, I'll stay and watch over her until she gets better."

Mable reassuringly patted Stella's arm. "Well, I'll be off now, dear. Archie will be wanting his tea when he gets back from the hospital." She made her way to the front door and stepped outside. "She'll be fine, you know. Women like her are as tough as old boots," she said as she walked down the short path and opened and closed the gate.

Stella not having been put in this sort of position before, didn't quite see that remark in the same light. She closed the front door…

An hour later, a young woman knocked on the door. "Hello, I'm Rosie, my Aunt Mable told me that you were expecting me," she said to Stella as she brushed past her and entered the house. She was pleasant enough but made no extra fuss of Ruth's situation. She knew what she had to do. After checking Ruth's pulse and seeing to her immediate needs, she gave her a sedative and told Stella to keep her as comfortable as she could. There was nothing else that she could do under the circumstances, so she left her to it.

With her arms crossed over her chest, Stella, her shoulders hunched, rested against the wall. She glanced around the quiet room—louder than ever, the clock ticked away. Her eyes blinked heavily as she took note of Ruth's paintings—they held serenity—something that Stella had forgotten about. The room itself was defined by feminal touches—lace edged linens covered the backs of the settee and the arm chair, a tall-standing lamp with a pink-pleated tiffany shade, stood in the corner of the room, and the floral patterned wallpaper in different shades of pink matched the plain-pink drapes.

•••

Stella had stayed with Ruth for the best part of the day. It had turned to early evening and she knew that it was too late for her to leave for the underground shelter. She also knew that she wouldn't leave Ruth alone and unconscious in the house. It was unnerving for her, as she hadn't experienced an air-raid without her family, nor from inside a house. She was worried how this was all going to pan out. She checked the cupboard under the stairs and cleared out the broom and a couple of boxes with bits-and-pieces in them. She then fetched some towels and a blanket from the airing cupboard and the cushions from the front room chairs. She made a comfortable little hideout. Then she found a torch in the kitchen sink-drawer and put that inside. Quickly checking outside to see just how dark it was getting, she knew that the air-raids would be starting fairly soon. It was time for her to move Ruth from the settee. She was glad that she had been sleeping all day, at least that way she hadn't felt too much in the way of pain. Holding her under her armpits, she lifted her up from the settee and dragged her backwards inside the small cupboard and laid her down on the make-shift bed, propping her head on the cushion. As soon as she was happy with her friend's condition, she closed the door and laid down on the cushions next to her, with the blanket covering them both. Now all she had to do was to wait it out until the sirens sounded off.

It had turned dark outside. The City of London was in complete darkness. All the streetlights were off and the houses blacked-out and hardly a soul out in the streets, apart from the Air-raid Wardens, who patrolled the streets and yelled out to anyone who had any kind of light showing from their home, 'Put those lights out.'

A Wartime Love
Shiralyn J. Lee

Stella laid in the darkness with one hand on Ruth's shoulder and the torch gripped tightly in her other hand. When the sirens finally sounded, her stomach turned over, as she felt the fear of the unknown flood right through her body. She sat up. Her back against the wall, her knees bent, her feet tucked in closely to her buttocks, she buried her face into her lap. Her hands, gripping at her skirt, became clammy, sweat escaped her pores—beading on her forehead trickled down her face, and her breathing became short bursts of pants, as she waited for the dreaded moment of attack.

Over the sounds of the sirens, she could hear the crump, crump, crump from the anti-attack guns, then, the distant rumbling drone, as the Luftwaffe planes flew closer. She put her hands over her ears in hopes that the sounds would disappear but it was of no use. The bomber planes flew closer and the drone grew louder. She felt the floor beneath her vibrate, caused by a bomb hitting a house in the neighbourhood. The incessant whistling sounds were around her, one after the other as the bombers off-loaded their UXB's, striking houses randomly and causing chaos everywhere.

Screams shadowed by the deafening booms, whaled from the house across the street. Stella had no idea what was happening to these people, only that she feared the worst for herself and her friend. Her tears of anguish flowed.

The drone grew louder and Stella knew that they were flying right over them. An explosion sounded, the house shook and then the screaming from the neighbour's house stopped. Stella felt sick, her stomach was in knots—her fear had been tested to its fullest—never before had she trembled as hard as she did. "Please stop, please stop, please stop," she chanted but her prayers went unanswered and the night went on regardless with bomb after bomb, dropped at will.

It became hard for her to breathe. Somehow the air seemed thick and heavy, as if it had abandoned her—her throat, dry, caused her to gag and inside her own head she was screaming but no sound had escaped her.

The strikes continued for hours and Stella had exhausted all thoughts of ever seeing the light of day again.

•••

Luckily for Stella and Ruth, the morning sun rose above the city. People, exhausted and fragile, emerged from the safety of the shelters. Once again, Hitler had failed to demoralise them. A shopkeeper swept the shattered glass from his doorstep—the displays of canned food all fallen and displaced from where they had been displayed in the shop-front window. But he still whistled as he cleaned up the mess—business would be open as usual.

At the moment that silence came about, Stella finally closed her sore tired eyes. She had no idea how long she had been asleep, when a frantic knocking sounded on Ruth's front door, startling her out of unconsciousness. She opened her eyes and at first, she wasn't sure what the noise was and a sinking feeling gript her. In her panicked mind, her eyes widened—she immediately looked at Ruth, who was still in a state of sedation.

"Stella!" Harriet shouted through the letterbox. "Stella, are you in there?"

Hearing her sister's voice, Stella opened the small door and crawled out. She rose to her knees and went to the front door, opening it, she threw her arms around her sister, relieved that they had all made it through the night. "Oh, my dearest, Harriet," she cried out.

"We were all worried sick about you," she said—her cheeks flushed with red. "I thought that Mum was surely going to die when you didn't show up at the underground. She didn't get a wink of sleep." She looked across the street behind her to where the neighbour's house was. Her eyes grew wide and her chin quivered as she absorbed just how close Stella had been to being killed. "Did that happen last night?"

Stella stepped out on to the doorstep and looked at what her sister was talking about. The house that she had heard screaming coming from had been levelled. Firemen had put the flames out and searched for any survivors but had only found two dead people, a man and a woman. Stella lowered her eyes in a state of sadness. She could hardly catch her breath. "I think I heard them screaming last night." A loud noise, initiated by some debris shifting, caused her to jolt.

Harriet sympathetically placed her hand on Stella's shoulder and stroked down her arm to indicate her empathy. She looked behind Stella. "Where's Ruth?" she asked.

Stella's head hung low—her eyes reddened, she glanced upwardly at her sister. "You had better come in." Harriet followed Stella inside the house and closed the door. Stella stopped at the foot of the stairs and grabbed hold of the bannister post—both hands cupped around the ball-shaped finial. She bowed her head and looked back over her shoulder. "Ruth lost her baby yesterday. I just couldn't leave her. One of her neighbours helped me and her niece, who's a nurse, gave her a sedative. Oh, dear Harriet, I didn't think I was ever going to see you again. It was just awful going through that." Tears ran down her cheeks as her body trembled—still feeling the effects of the previous terrifying hours.

Harriet dropped her bag on the ground and rushed to hug her sister—embracing her from behind, she snuggled her head against Stella's back. "We all feared the worst for you. Daddy said I was to bring you back home immediately and that I wasn't to accept the word no from you either."

Stella let out a whimper. She took hold of Harriet's hand and showed her the sick woman who could not be moved. Harriet knew that she would be fighting a losing argument and that she would be returning home without her sister whilst Ruth was in this state.

"I can't leave her, Harriet."

Harriet slapped her hand over her mouth. "What are you going to do?" she asked.

Stella shook her head and shrugged her shoulders. "I went through hell last night but Ruth needs me and until she's well enough to move, I have no choice but to stay with her. She gripped hold of one of the staircase spindles and rested her head against it. Torrential tears flowed and then she let out an almighty cry.

A Wartime Love
Shiralyn J. Lee

Harriet began to panic for her. She didn't want to leave her sister in this state. "Wait! I think I may have a solution." She remembered seeing an abandoned wheelchair a short walk from Ruth's house. Not leaving any time to explain, she ran out of the house and disappeared out of the Terrace. A few moments later, she returned with the wheelchair in question. A proud smile broke across her face as she opened the gate and wheeled it up the font path to the door. "We can put her in this and then take her to the underground, where we can all be safe."

Stella, propped against the open door, was more than grateful for her sister's find. Her stiffened stance relaxed—she unfolded her crossed arms and even managed a slight half-smile, in respect of her sister's find.

As Harriet brought it inside the house, a distant drone could be heard in the air. Stella moved away from the door, taking a step back inside—her eyes grew large, filled with fear. She hadn't prepared herself to go through another attack so soon after the last. Harriet stopped dead in the hallway, she turned her head slowly to check with Stella that she was hearing the same noise. For a brief moment, the two sisters were fearful for their lives. But as the drone grew closer, it was discovered that a squadron of Spitfires were flying overhead and they were on their way to bomb the enemy land…Germany. People of all ages went out into the streets and cheered as they watched their heroes on their way to fight for their country. It was a welcomed, magnificent sight.

It brought a smile to Harriet's face and for the first time in a while, her huge doe-eyes were filled with hope. "We're going to win this war, aren't we? Hitler can't keep bombing us forever, can he? Surely he's going to run out of bombs soon enough?"

Stella reached for the brass latch and closed the door. A long sigh left her. She turned around to look at Harriet and gave her a brave smile, covering up her real feelings—fear that this war would not end well for her and her kind.

Chapter Five

Ruth regained consciousness and opened her eyes. She laid still, looking up at the low ceiling above her— unsure of where she was for a moment. She could hear voices coming from one of the rooms—they were mumbled, making it hard for her to hear what they were saying. She tried to move but pain caused her to yelp out. She held her hand over her stomach, tugging at her blouse as the agony ran through her. Tears fell from the sides of her eyes and trickled into her hairline.

Stella, seated in the armchair, her legs crossed at the ankles and her slender feet out of her shoes, held a rose-patterned china cup, filled with tea, to her lips and the saucer rested in the open-palm of her other hand. Harriet, her hands clasped behind her back, stood in front of the fireplace admiring the beautiful paintings that Ruth had mounted on the wall. Hearing Ruth's woeful cry, they both rushed out of the front room to the hallway cupboard, dropping to their knees to peer inside.

A Wartime Love
Shiralyn J. Lee

Ruth winced. She turned her head to look at them. The gash on her forehead had caused a bump and deep bruising—her throat was dry. "What happened to me...why am I in here?" she mumbled through her breath.

Stella crawled inside the cupboard and knelt at Ruth's side, looking her over from her head to her feet. "You're in pain." She carefully picked up her hand—clasping it gently between her palms—her voice a mere trace of its usual tone, she hesitantly informed her about her experience. "You've been through a terrible ordeal."

Drawing in a long breath, Ruth sluggishly closed her eyes and reluctantly thought back to the previous day. As the realisation sank in that she'd lost her baby, she trembled convulsively—tears pooled in her dark-eyes. She tried to force herself from shedding them but with one lingered blink, they dissolved and seeped from the outer corners of her eyes. "What's wrong with me?" she wept.

"Are you able to move at all?" Harriet pitifully interrupted. "We're going to take you home with us, aren't we Stella?" Her eyes lifted from Ruth's pained guise and connected with Stella's anguished stare.

Stella forced a charitable smile and slowly nodded in agreement.

Ruth paled in colour as she tried to pull herself up—yelping as the pain hit with force.

"Let me help you," Stella, still panicked, offered. She crawled behind Ruth's head and with her hands tucked into her armpits, she slowly pulled her up into a sitting position—propping her up into the crevice of her own lap and upper body. "I'm going to drag you out of here."

Ruth held her breath while Stella carefully pulled her backwards, with Harriet—her voice aflutter, guiding her out into the hallway. Once they had brought her out into the open, they hoisted her up—one sister on each side of Ruth, and settled her into the wheelchair.

"Splendid," Harriet said, proud that she'd found the abandoned item.

With her head lowered, Ruth glanced sideways at her saviours, then turned her head away, believing that she had overly concerned them with her troubles. Feeling shamed, she closed her eyes tightly. "I don't want to cause any bother to either of you, or your kind family. Surely I must be a burden to you all right now?" She gripped her skirt and tugged nervously at the material—her knuckles whitened from the intensity.

A Wartime Love
Shiralyn J. Lee

Harriet's pupils' dilated. She crossed her arms over her chest and dropped one hip slightly—resting her weight mainly on one leg. "What a load of bloody nonsense," she said firmly. "I know how my sister is and she would not have it any other flipping way. Do you think that she would have left you last night during that raid? We were all worried as hell, especially Mummy and Daddy."

"Harriet!!" Stella scorned. "Where on earth did you learn such foul language?"

Harriet tilted her head and gave a half-smug smile. "Around," she said. Her naturally rosy cheeks filled out as her smile turned into a childish giggle.

Hearing that Stella had stayed at her side, Ruth looked sharply at her. "You…you stayed with me?" She released her skirt from her tense grip—stretching her fingers to bring the tingling sensation back into them. She relaxed her shoulders and then brushed her hands over her skirt.

Stella moved behind the wheelchair and took hold of the handles. "Let's get a move on, shall we?" With Ruth unable to see her, she smiled gracefully to herself. She pushed the chair forwards towards the door.

Harriet bolted to the door and unlatched it. Before she fully opened it, she looked back over her shoulder

A Wartime Love
Shiralyn J. Lee

at the others. Her eyes dropped their gaze. "It's pretty nightmarish out there," she sadly told them. "Oh wait! Let me get your blanket…"

…"My handbag, please don't forget that," Ruth called after Harriet as she raced around the house looking for any other personal artefacts that might be needed.

Harriet gathered Ruth's belongings together and placed them inside a cotton canvas bag. She slung it over her shoulder and then stood at the door, holding it open, while Stella pushed Ruth's wheelchair out onto the front path.

Even though the effects of smoke still drifted in the air with the light breeze, and the smell of burnt wood and charred belongings lingered, pigeons, blue-tits, magpies and robins, were still significant in numbers. Their survival had proven to be no less than miraculous throughout the bombings—their chirps and songs did not go unnoticed by the local people.

It was an uncomfortable journey for Ruth. She bravely kept her pain secretive whilst Harriet walked on slightly ahead of them, kicking away pieces of broken bricks and cindered-wood. Stella tried her best not to wheel over too much of the debris—she knew that Ruth would be suffering with discomfort.

A Wartime Love
Shiralyn J. Lee

Once again, their city was in an eerie state of destruction. Where many houses had been destroyed, others were left in untouched conditions, or with just slight evidence of rubble that had been blown their way. Smoke rose from where the flames had been put out, and even though the day itself was filled with glorious sunshine and very few white clouds, the citizens in the thick of the destruction were not privy to it. Instead, they bravely carried on under the cloud of opaque-grey and the smell of charred wood that carried with the current of air.

A black Labrador dog stood at the foot of nothing more than what could be described as a pile of broken bricks. It barked as it watched the firemen search through it, looking for survivors. Perhaps it was waiting for its master to be found, or it was barking because it knew that there was someone beneath the rubble still barely alive—perhaps.

But life still went on as normally as it possibly could. The people of London were not broken—not yet, or if they were, they were not allowing the enemy any joy in seeing it.

The one thing that Ruth was grateful for, was that it was only a short journey to where Stella lived. She clenched her fists and kept them hidden at her sides, away from Stella. She knew that she had to be brave and that the sooner they were in the safety of her home, the sooner this pained ordeal would be over.

Harriet turned around to check on her sister and Ruth. She could see that Ruth was in a lot of discomfort with each bump and wobble caused by the wreckage. "Dearest, Ruth, you are the bravest person. It won't be long now, I promise."

Seeing that Harriet was being compassionate, Ruth bravely managed to produce a smile. In a low subdued tone she replied to her concern. "I will be okay."

Stella, determined to end their venture as quickly as possible, let go of one of the handles and placed the flat of her palm on Ruth's shoulder. With empathy, she lightly patted it. Ruth unclenched her fist. Her hand found its way to her shoulder and appreciatively, she placed it on top of Stella's hand—their friendship had been bonded for life.

•••

Harriet slipped the strap of her handbag from her shoulder and fumbled around inside for her house keys. Grabbing them, she opened the front door and stepped inside to the hallway. "Mummy, Daddy, are you home? I've brought Stella home and Ruth's with her too."

A Wartime Love
Shiralyn J. Lee

Wiping her hands on a tea-towel, their mother walked out from the kitchen—her shrill—ear piercing, when she saw that Stella had returned home safe.

Hearing the commotion, their father—pipe in his mouth, emerged from the front room. His arms crossed over his chest—his shoulders pushed back to straighten his stance, he clinched his jaw. Lines covered his forehead, as his eyebrows hooded over his narrowed eyes. "I don't doubt for a moment that you don't already know how disappointed I am in you, Stella. Your mother and I were quite put out by your lack of presence last night. I don't know if it was an act of stupidity, or an act of bravery, that you did but you would be making a wise choice to not do that again." He sucked on the mouthpiece of his pipe—a puff of smoke escaped.

Stella's face turned crimson. She connected her gaze with her mother's foreboding eyes and then gradually looked at her father, whose objecting glare made her realise that she had foolishly dismissed her family during such a dire time. She closed her eyes and turned her head away—her voice quiet—"I'm so sorry, Daddy."

Ruth knew that Stella had bravely risked her life to stay with her. She gave a polite cough to interrupt the scornful words from hurting Stella even further. "Your daughter is a hero to me," she said softly. "If it wasn't for her bravery, I might very-well be dead right now. I apologise if I seem to come across a little curt but it wasn't exactly pleasant for her. I think that we should all be thankful for her quick-thinking actions."

"You're quite right, dear," Stella's mother piped up. "We were just thinking about our own selfish feelings." She stepped forward towards Ruth. Now then, let me take a look at that nasty bump and cut on your head."

Stella gave a short shake of her head to alert her mother that it wasn't a good idea to bring Ruth's injury up. Her mother casually reeled back and shook her head in unison with her daughter's.

Ruth brushed her fingers over her injury. "It's quite all right, Stella. I have to be brave about it all." She patted Stella's hand—a gesture that went down well with Stella.

Stella's mother headed towards the kitchen—stopping at the doorway she looked back and gave a motherly smile to the girls. "Well, I've made a lovely leek pudding. It should just about be ready now, so come on through and I'll get us all something to eat before we have to leave again for the underground."

•••

A Wartime Love
Shiralyn J. Lee

That night, the raids, as expected, came again. The Baxter's and Ruth, along with relentless others, slept on the cold concrete platforms of the underground station. Many people were worn-out through the stress, some even wore black armbands, marking the loss of a close loved one.

Stella made Ruth as comfortable as possible by ruffling extra blankets beneath her. She had taken her own pillow from her bed and given it to Ruth to use.

"How is your friend doing, dear?" her mother asked.

Stella, sat with her back against the tiled wall, looked over at Ruth, who was on her side, in a deep sleep. "I think she'll be fine," she whispered back.

Harriet huddled up to Stella on her other side. She rested her head on her shoulder—her coat pulled tightly around her, she pulled her blanket up to cover her entire body and the lower portion of her face. She wore her mittens and a woollen scarf that her mother had knitted her for the previous Christmas. "I'm so cold, Stella. I want to be home in my nice comfy warm bed, not in here, shivering and scared."

Stella placed her arm around her sister—her cheek pressed into the top of Harriet's head—her eyes saddened by her thoughts. She let out a lingered heavy sigh. "I'm sure that we all do, sweet Harriet." She

A Wartime Love
Shiralyn J. Lee

closed her eyes—the edges of her lids laced with tears that she fought to hold back.

Doris and Joan were seated next to Harriet. They had overheard their sisters' conversation, which saddened them both. Joan picked up Doris's hand and placed it onto her lap, squeezing it for assurance. The whites of her eyes had turned red from her developing salty tears, her induced smile—brittle.

Doris sucked on her lower lip, biting down on it with her teeth to prevent herself from crying.

Each of the sisters' glanced around at the display of people forced into sleeping like rats huddled in a corner. A cough here and there, echoed, an unsettled baby cried, an elderly man sat hunched against the wall—his flat-cap in his hand, pressed against his face, so that his tears wouldn't be seen—every single one of these people had a personal story to tell about death and ruination.

Meanwhile, for continuous hours, London continued to withstand the turbulent attacks above them. Hitler's message was clearly being heard and felt by the recipients.

Prayer—prayer gave them hope, dignity and strength to carry on. Prayer gave them knowledge. Prayer was all they had, that Hitler couldn't take away from them…

•••

The following morning, for many, it was work as usual. One thing that Hitler couldn't break, was the people's strength—he was infuriated by their tolerance, something that he had failed to consider in the beginning. His anger grew. It grew so much, that instead of using his knowledge for war tactics, he used his frustration to dictate his next moves—each time, these moves proving to be less effective than he had desired.

With Harriet taking care of her, Ruth had gone home with Stella's family. Stella had had no choice but to go to work.

The devastation was widespread. Houses looked like they had been sliced in half. Bedroom floors jutted out—hanging by a thread. There were some with wardrobes, beds and chests of drawers, all still perfectly in place. Curtains flapped, as the breeze moved them, and in the lower portion of the houses, slivers of glass sparkled, as pockets of sun rays caught their reflection. Brick dust covered everything in its path and still lingered in the air, being breathed in and tasted by those who had to walk in close proximity, some sneezing, some coughing, others covering their mouths with their coats, or handkerchiefs. But there was one thing that everyone had that was identical to each other—the desolate look in their eyes. Only sadness filled them—nothing else. It wouldn't matter who they were, or how old they were, their eyes said it all.

•••

Stella arrived safely at the school. The children were in their usual small groups. The girls playing hopscotch and skipping with ropes. The boys playing marbles and conkers, and no doubt, discussing the recent havoc that had been caused by the bombing.

Mr. Fletcher stood in the middle of the playground and blew the whistle at 8.58a.m. The children stopped playing and formed rows for their assigned class and then at 9a.m. were led away into the school by their class teacher.

•••

Stella sat at her desk—the blackboard with chalked lines and alphabet letters, behind her. On the desk in front of her, the register book—it was open. She held a pencil in her hand, reading out the name of each child, she wrote a tick mark next to those who were in attendance and a cross next to those who were not.

"Thomas Peters?" she called out, looking down at his name with the pencil hovering over it.

"Yes, Miss," the young voice answered.

"Kevin Aldercock?"

A cheeky red-faced boy in grey shorts and a knitted grey vest-top over his short-sleeved shirt, swung his legs and grinned. Picking his nose, he responded. "Yes, Miss."

"Amelia Harrington?" … "Amelia Harrington?"… The silence caused Stella to stare at her name in the book—the pencil lead just touching the paper, ready to mark it. She placed the pencil down and looked up from the register book, directing her gaze at each child in the classroom. The children looked around at each other and then at her. Most of them shrugged their little shoulders, not knowing why Amelia was absent from school. "Has anyone seen Amelia Harrington?" she asked—her tone hushed. Deep down, she knew the possible outcome of this little girl. Admitting it, would make it real.

"She's dead, Miss," Thomas Peters said sadly, looking over his shoulder at the girl's empty chair.

Stella held her hand over her mouth—she swallowed hard. The last image of that little girl, was of her crying over her having head lice. Stella stared at her empty desk and chair. Her attention was then drawn to another empty seat. She didn't want to ask…"Has anyone seen Christopher Hammond?"

"He's dead too, Miss. The Jerrys killed him, and his parents, last night," Steven Winchester informed her. "They didn't get his dog, though, Miss. My dad said that it was barking in the street for hours this morning."

With a sickened feeling in the pit of her stomach, Stella had to remain calm. Her body trembled internally, her skin tone—washed out. She continued her task of calling out the children's names, and drew a pencil tick in the book for the ones who answered her call. She then got up from her chair and paced around the classroom, checking the fronts and backs of each child's hands—ensuring their cleanliness. Normality had to remain.

A short while later, Mrs. Davis's voice travelled through the corridor. It grated on Stella's mind. She was furious that this woman could still remain as callous, even with the loss of a few children from her class. Stella rose from her chair and went over to the door. She looked back at the children, who were writing down their alphabets. "Carry on working, I shall just be a short moment." Feeling vexed, she then left the classroom and entered Mrs. Davis's. She stood with her arms crossed—the middle finger of her right hand tapped irritably on her lower left arm, rhythmically with her tapping foot. "Could I have a word with you in the corridor?" she asked her. Turning, and heading back out through the door before she'd even received a reply.

Mrs. Davis peered over her glasses and moved away from the blackboard, where a young boy was standing next to her. With a piece of white chalk, he was writing the word 'displease' over and over again, due to misspelling it earlier. No doubt, this was who Mrs. Davis had been screaming at a few moments ago. She followed Stella out into the corridor. Her eyes narrowed with suspicion. Each wrinkle around her mouth exaggerated by her scowling pursed lips. The overly-large mole on her chin, clustered with white facial hairs, became more prominent and her priggish stance stiffened, waiting for her nemesis to speak. Her voice pitched with displeasure—"Well, what is it?"

Stella's usual paled face, flushed with crimson. She let out a long breath. "I'm going to ask you this as one teacher to another. But would you please stop your incessant yelling at the children in your class? I hear it day after day from my classroom and it just goes right through me, so I can only imagine what it does to those poor children, who are doing their best under these circumstances. I do understand that you have the old system installed inside you but these children are undergoing a major catastrophe, just as we all are."

Mrs. Davis turned her head slightly away—looking at Stella with a sideways glance, she placed her bony hands on her hips—her long fingernails digging deep into her jacket. And with her nose scrunched up, she compared to that of a ferret's face. "May I remind you that I have been teaching for forty-five years and never once have I had to endure such rude behaviour from another teacher, especially one who is still wet behind the ears."

"Mrs. Davis, your insults do not go far with me. I think I can safely speak for all of the other teachers too, when I say to you that your behaviour is far beyond acceptable. Now please, would you keep your foul temper under control and let some of the other classes focus on their own work, and not have to be interrupted every time that you feel one of your pupils has made a spelling mistake." Stella held her nose high and turned quickly to go back inside her own classroom but as she was about to open the door, Mrs. Davis had one last insult to make.

"No wonder you and your snivelling sisters can't get yourselves a decent man to settle down with. Being as outspoken as you all are, I'm sure that you'll all be living in that house together in your old ages, looking back over the years that you all wasted with your pathetic little lives."

Her words hit hard with Stella. Insulting her was one thing, Stella could easily defend herself but insulting her sisters, was a different matter altogether. She turned around to take a good look at the old wrinkly woman, who was standing with her arms crossed tightly over her chest—her grey plaited hair that had been tied up on top of her head—her thin rimmed glasses that sat at the end of her long thin nose and her skin—there could be no paler skin than her insipid looking flesh. "You dare to insult my family, and yet you stand here in front of me, looking as you do, and may I add, with no husband to mention of. Our country is at war, or hadn't you noticed that? Have a little sense of compassion, at least." She opened the door collectedly. As calmly as she had left the classroom, she entered it gracefully. The children still had their heads down, writing their A, B, C's with their pencils. Stella walked around the class, looking over the children's shoulders to see if they truly were writing. She was pleased with the result. She walked back to her desk, where she seated herself quietly in her chair—her elbows propped on the desk, with her chin lightly rested on her hands—her eyes moving slowly around the room, catching a look at each child. "Now, where were we?" She glanced sideways to the door, to see Mrs. Davis still standing in the corridor, glaring at her. Stella gave her a half-grin, then arched her brow slyly, as a mark of triumph. She nodded her head once, it was her way of acknowledging her antagonist.

Mrs. Davis—her jaw clenched, her eyes beady, turned away and went back inside her own classroom. Stella felt proud of herself for finally standing up to that old witch but she couldn't allow the children to see her glee, so she kept her head low and pretended that she was reading through a book. She looked up at the pupils when she heard a couple of the boys in the back of the class, muttering amongst themselves. They seemed engrossed in whatever it was that they were talking about. Stella rose from her chair and pushed it away from her with the backs of her legs. She roamed over to the boys' desks, where she stood behind them for a moment, listening to them converse.

"I bet the piece I found is better than yours," Thomas, his shoulders hunched, his head down low, said to Arnold Epps, who was sat at a desk in the row next to him.

Arnold opened the top of his desk and produced a piece of shrapnel from an ack ack shell. His grin was that of quite an achievement.

Stella reached over Arnold and tapped the open desk with her pencil. "It would be wise to put that back inside your desk, Arnold, and continue with what you are here for." Standing passively, she turned her attention to Thomas. "The same goes for you too, Thomas."

Thomas sucked in his cheeks, sat up straight, with his back stiffened and clasped his hands together on top of his desk, like a perfect angel. "Yes, Miss," he answered.

Arnold—his face red from being rattled, placed the shrapnel back in his desk and closed the top down. "Sorry, Miss," he said, apologetically.

A Wartime Love
Shiralyn J. Lee

Chapter Six

May 11th 1941. After a merciless 57 day-and-night campaign of bombing raids over London, and then months of sporadic attacks across the United Kingdom, attacking Portsmouth, Plymouth, Bristol, Southampton, Liverpool, Glasgow and many other key areas, Hitler called off the incessant raids and turned his attention to Russia. But in the midst of the continued attacks, Hitler had overlooked a vital mistake. Concentrating on killing the citizens of London and bombing major ports, Britain had been able to rebuild its defence system. Factories had been turned into military production lines, women were trained in men's jobs, making homeland production invaluable. The Brits were able to amass their air-defence, ground observation, gunnery, bomber planes and Spitfires. Searchlights were better equipped to seek out enemy planes approaching, as their brilliant blue/white lights beamed on and through the clouds. Added to them was a gun pit, a spotter chair and field telephones. Even though many of these land guns hardly hit a target, their mere existence and sounds of fire were of comfort to the citizens. Civil defence grew in numbers. More volunteers did their bit in becoming Home Guards, Observer Corps, A.R.P's. Women in the WVS set up mobile canteens, providing food and drink around the clock to A.R.P wardens and firemen, which in turn, placed them, as unsung heroes, in immediate danger. They also looked after the injured and those who had been made homeless. These women had gone from housewives, and daughters, who had helped their mothers around the house, to become women of great courage, who risked their lives every day.

Government posters were placed everywhere:

'Save Fuel!'

'Make do and mend!'

'Buy savings stamps!'

'Cough's and Sneeze's Spread Diseases!'

This was part of the plan to stop the country from falling on its knees—it worked. Even hemlines of skirts became shorter in order to save on material, gravy browning was used to colour bare legs and a straight line drawn down the backs of legs, to give the impression that stockings were being worn. The women had found a way to keep fashion as great as ever.

•••

A Wartime Love
Shiralyn J. Lee

Ruth had recovered from the loss of her unborn baby. She had spent much time in the association of Stella and the Baxter family—enjoying their company, and they in return, enjoyed hers. Periodically, Stella visited Ruth at her house, where this became far more regular, as they grew to know each other.

Joan and William had been able to enjoy a few evenings out together, before he was deployed with his army regiment to fight against Germany on their land. Her excitement of being engaged to him, gave the family some sort of blissful joy for once. She even wore a sweetheart lapel badge in the way of miniature RAF Wings, to signify her honour towards her fiancé.

Doris had volunteered as an A.R.P and Harriet was working in a military production factory. In such a short space of time, the Baxter household had changed, as had many others had but still, they remained strong and determined.

•••

Stella was with Ruth at her house, helping her out with doing the laundry, as Monday was laundry day. Ruth scrubbed her dress and bedsheets on the tin washboard and Stella rinsed them out for her and then Ruth squeezed them through the mangle, turning the handle for the two rollers to wring the water out. She then hung them over the wooden clothes horse and aired them dry in front of the fire that Stella had lit for her.

They had bought apples and a brisket joint with their ration coupons. After cooking the joint, Stella had peeled and sliced the apples, then dried them out by hooping them on sticks and placing them in the warm oven for a couple of hours.

They were sat in the front room drinking a cup of tea, when they heard the sound of a motorbike approaching outside. The hairs on Ruth's neck stood up. This was not a sound that anyone wanted to hear coming down their street. It was a heart stopping moment for anyone, and curtains twitched in each house to see where the motorbike would stop. Ruth trembled, as the splutter of the exhaust grew louder. Her cup tinkered on its saucer, spilling some tea, as she placed it down on the side table. Stella got up from her seat to look out of the window, where she saw a young man on a motorbike stop outside of Ruth's house. This could only mean one thing. That someone she was close to, was either missing in action, or dead. The young man, who worked for the Post Office Telegram Service, opened Ruth's gate—his head hung low, he wrapped his knuckles on her front door. Holding a telegram in his hand, he waited for her to answer—

neighbours stood at their front room windows with mixed emotions, grateful that he wasn't knocking on their door but saddened by the fact that he was knocking on someone else's that they knew of.

Ruth—her dark-eyes focused on Stella, who in turn, couldn't look at her, rose slowly from her seat, gradually edging her way to the front door. She knew of only one person this could be about—her husband. Holding her breath—her eyes focused on the floor, she gripped the latch with both hands. Just for a short moment, she paused, knowing that delaying whatever it was, would give her a few more seconds of existing without pain. Opening the front door, her eyes lifted from their anxious stare, they met with the young boy's.

Stroking the side of his nose with his forefinger—his head stable, his eyes, extended in their gaze wandered over to the window, where Stella held back the lace curtain. He had no words of comfort for her, as he handed over the telegram. He removed his hat and again lowered his head. His tone of voice flat, "I'm so sorry to have to hand you this," he said.

Ruth felt the wedding band on her finger instantly tighten, making her even more aware of Clifford's predicament. She fidgeted with it—twisting it nervously—her hands trembled.

A Wartime Love
Shiralyn J. Lee

The young man turned and walked away. Starting his motorbike up, he rode off to the next poor unsuspecting loved one. Ruth could see the curtains moving in the houses adjacent to hers—there was nothing, absolutely nothing, that could prepare anyone for these telegrams. She closed the door. With the telegram held tightly in her grip, she collapsed to the floor, crying out her tears of pain.

Stella, hearing the tumultuous cry, rushed to her rescue and lifted her up from the floor—taking her to the front room, where she sat her down on the settee. She crouched down on the carpet at her knees and coaxed her to sip some tea before she opened the telegram. Ruth couldn't bear to open it. She handed it over to Stella. "Please," she whimpered.

Holding the sealed envelope, Stella looked down at it—her eyes darting over the print. "Are you absolutely sure that you want me to read this?" she asked her. Ruth drew in her lips, biting them between her teeth. She nodded bravely. Stella opened the sealed telegram and read out the words that Ruth's husband, Clifford Arnold, was missing in action. This was a bitter-sweet message, as at least he wasn't being reported as dead, not that this telegram didn't mean that he wasn't. Missing, didn't give any better hope to those on homeland, it just intensified their stress, as not knowing, played games with people's thoughts—Ruth's thoughts were no exception. "I'm so sorry, Ruth," Stella said, reaching her hand out to take Ruth's. The unknowing connection, surprisingly soothing to both of them. She looked over the open palm, then placed it to her lips—her kiss, a light trace that caused Ruth to shiver.

Ruth moved her gaze from Stella, to the window—the endless depth of darkness in her pain-filled eyes, intensified by the pooling tears about to fall. "I seem to attract the worst, don't I?"

"No you don't, my sweet dearest Ruth." Stella, her body drooped, let out a heavy sigh. She leaned forward and placed her head on Ruth's lap—her tears formed and rolled down the side of her face, dripping onto Ruth's skirt. "You are the kindest, sweetest person that I've ever met outside of my family."

Ruth lifted her hand, hovering it over Stella's head. Her fingers bent, she retracted it. "Why do you say that? I've brought you and your family so much misery with my own woes."

"Nonsense. They adore you…I adore you." Stella wiped her eyes with her sleeve, then lifted her head from Ruth's lap. Her nose dripping, she brushed her hand beneath it, then stood up. "I'm so sorry, I'm being selfish. Perhaps I should leave and give you some time to process your news." Embarrassed by her words, she headed for the door.

Ruth rose immediately from the settee and reached out for Stella's hand—pulling her back towards her. They stood facing each other—Ruth on one side of the door frame and Stella on the other. "I'm so confused. My heart pounds whenever I'm near you, and yet, I'm standing here with the news that my husband is missing. What's wrong with me, Stella?" She rested her forehead against Stella's—all Stella could do, was stare directly into her eyes. "Please don't leave, Stella," she whispered to her.

Stella tilted her head, her closed mouth melted into a smile. "I won't. If you want me to stay, then I will."

Ruth took hold of Stella's hand and clasped their fingers together. "I want you to stay. I'm so scared of being alone but I'm more afraid of you walking out of that door and never returning. I cannot lose you from my life…I need you, Stella, I really need you."

Stella rested her cheek on Ruth's shoulder and then nuzzled her face into her neck. Ruth released her hand from Stella's and placed it on the small of her back, pulling her in close to her—both bodies trembled, as they pressed firmly against each other's. Stella placed

A Wartime Love
Shiralyn J. Lee

her hands on Ruth's tiny waist, her fingers awkwardly fumbled over the fabric of her clothing. She gradually moved her face away from Ruth's shoulder—her lips brushing over Ruth's soft peachy skin as she nervously made her way towards her mouth.

Ruth could feel Stella's warm breath sweep over the side of her face—her breathing became erratic, as she apprehensively waited for their first kiss.

Their lips met just briefly. Stella pulled away to assure herself that this was what Ruth wanted, as well as her. Not only did she smile with her mouth—her pale-green eyes gave away just how jubilant she was actually feeling. "I've never kissed anyone before," she whispered.

Ruth's chin quivered, as she broke a brittle smile. She closed her eyes and parted her lips, moving in slowly to kiss Stella's.

Stella closed her eyes. A tingling sensation fluttered through her stomach, her eyelids flickered, as she nervously tried to keep them closed. The palms of her hands became clammy, as she awkwardly brushed them over Ruth's satin blouse—not knowing exactly where to place them. As their mouth's parted, both women blushingly looked downwards.

"I've never kissed a woman before," Ruth said softly. She took hold of Stella's hand and looked towards the top of the stairs.

Stella's face filled with red, as she blushed. Her breathing became heavy and loud—her nostrils flared, giving away the fact that she was taken by both, desire and curiosity.

•••

Stella laid on her stomach, with her chin cupped in the palms of her hands—her elbows dug deep into the mattress and her knees bent with her feet in the air behind her. She had kicked the bedspread away from her—she was naked. She watched Ruth as she slept—her hair spread over her pillow—her hand, with her fingers slightly bent, placed next to her face. It was a picturesque moment for Stella—one that she would never forget.

The dimly lit lamp on the table, on Stella's side of the bed, offered minimal light, causing Ruth's image to be mainly covered by shadows. Stella held her hand over Ruth's stomach. She wanted to touch her again—to feel that excitement of energy run through her veins but she also wanted to watch her sleep, as she knew that it was the only way that she could be offered any peace in her thoughts. She carefully retracted her hand.

A Wartime Love
Shiralyn J. Lee

•••

Ruth woke to the smell of toast wafting upstairs from the kitchen. She sat up, to find that Stella wasn't by her side. Sliding out of bed, she put on her silk robe, tied the ribbon-belt in a bow at the front and made her way down to the kitchen, where she found Stella humming to herself. She was spreading plum jam thinly over the warm-buttered toast. Ruth stood behind her and placed her hands around her waist—her face nestled into the back of Stella's neck.

Stella's angelic smile radiated across her face. Still holding the toast in one hand and the knife in the other, she turned to give Ruth a light peck on her cheek. "Hello," she said in a sheepishly quiet voice.

Ruth kissed the tip of Stella's nose. "Hello back," she replied unashamedly.

Amidst a country filled with horrors of war, the one place that both of these women felt safe, was in each other's soft embrace. It was as though life around them had momentarily stopped.

Stella offered a slice of toast into Ruth's mouth—Ruth took a bite out of it. "Is this the jam that your mother made?"

Stella licked her finger, where the jam had dripped.

"Yes it is."

Ruth took a second bite. With her mouth full, she said, "This is good, she really knows how to cook."

With it being a fairly warm day, Stella had opened the back door and the window above the kitchen sink, to allow the natural daylight to filter through.

The sound of the RAF fighters flying overhead, gave an extra comfort to those who were on the ground, looking up at them. Another attack on Germany gave the citizens of England a new hope—one that would give them the belief that the war would be over with—one they would win, meaning life would return back to normal.

But the war continued on, and Europe was at the centre of the world's attention…that was, until December 7th. Japan had committed the most unthinkable act on America. They had bombed Pearl Harbour in a surprise attack, which in turn, killed and injured thousands of unsuspecting people. The following day, America declared war on Japan, bridging their alliance with Britain.

Chapter Seven

Stella and Ruth had gone to visit Stella's family. Now that she spent most of her time at Ruth's house, she felt as though she had not been home enough to assure them that she was in safe hands.

They sat at the kitchen table, while Stella's mother ground up some fresh pork meat in the meat grinder. "I'm going to make a lovely cottage pie today," she told them. "Your favourite, hey, Stella."

Discretely touching Ruth's leg with her bare foot, Stella—her elbows on the table, her chin rested in the palms of her hands, smiled at her mother. "It's been a while since we had that, Mum."

Her mother stopped feeding the meat through the grinder. She looked over her shoulder at the pair, who were not paying too much attention to what she was doing. "And by the looks of your skinny body, I'd say that you could do with an extra helping, my dear. The same goes for you too, Ruth. Are you girls not eating properly?"

A Wartime Love
Shiralyn J. Lee

Ruth mimicked Stella by placing her elbows on the edge of the table—resting her chin in her fisted hands. Her eyes—glazed with ravishment, focused on Stella. To her, she wasn't skinny, or scrawny, or anything of the like. To her, she was perfect. She released a subtle smile, just enough for Stella to engage in the allure of her charm. Her gaze slowly shifted sideways from Stella, over to her mother. "Yes, Mrs. Baxter. We're both eating fine."

"Well, I'm certainly glad to hear that. I can't go worrying about you both not looking after yourselves, now can I?"

•••

It was late afternoon. Harriet, now volunteering as an ARP, arrived home. She was excited and raced into the kitchen. "There's a load of American troops just arrived in the country. I've just seen some of them driving Jeeps, and one of them even had the cheek to whistle at me. Their uniforms are so swish. Stella, perhaps you and Ruth should join me and Doris in the pub for a drink tonight? I'm sure they'll be in there, if they're anything like our boys. Oh, Stella, please say you will."

Stella looked across the table at Ruth—her gaze—one of, 'oh my god what should we do?' was understood by its receiver. She then turned her gaze back to Harriet, who was rambling on about how the American's were going to help Britain win the war and how Hitler was going to regret ever sending his wretched planes over. Excited, she paced the kitchen, picking out a tea cup and then turned around to the table, picked up the tea pot and poured the hot tea into her cup. She guzzled loudly on it, as her elation about the troops had made her a little breathless. "You know, Ruth, Joan and Doris used to tease Stella about becoming an old spinster. Perhaps we'll all find ourselves a nice American soldier to marry, wouldn't that be a hoot."

"Harriet, dearest, you do like to dream," her mother giggled.

Harriet sat at the table with her sister and her friend. She crossed her one leg over the other and swung it— displaying her happy mood. "Well, I'm sure that you and Daddy don't want us all living here forever, now do you, Mummy?"

"Well, I'm certain that I shall shed a tear, or two, each time one of my girls leaves this house, I don't doubt that. Look at Stella here, we hardly ever see her these days and that's not meant as anything towards you, Ruth. I'm sure you're just as lonely in that house of yours. Have you heard anymore news about your husband, dear?"

Dropping her shoulders—her face lowered, Ruth hesitantly shook her head. Biting her lower lip between her teeth, she raised her eyes to see if Stella was looking—she was.

Although Ruth was technically a married woman, Stella knew that she had a lesser role to play as far as, 'marital-law', was concerned. She chose to answer her mother's question for her lover. "He's still missing, Mummy." She reached out to Ruth's arm and stroked it—a sign of sympathy in her family's eyes.

Her mother wrapped a tea-towel around the handle of the kettle—it had just boiled on the cooker top. She carried it over to the table and poured the hot water into the tea pot. "Well that's just terrible. You must be thinking all sorts, not knowing where he is?" she asked.

A loud sigh left Ruth's mouth. "Yes."

Stella pinched the edge of Ruth's saucer and slid it, with the cup tinkering, across the table towards her. "Well, I for one think we should have another cup of tea. Ruth?"

The back door opened and Stella's father entered. He took off his shoes and removed his cap before walking across the kitchen. "They've cleared some bombed areas out and turned them into allotments. I've been giving a hand this afternoon. That was until a rabble of American troops drove past us, all whistling at every young woman that they came across. Disgraceful behaviour. If you ask me, they're all overpaid, oversexed and over here."

Harriet looked up at her father. "Oh, Daddy, now don't be too brash to judge them. I'm sure there's plenty of good men amongst them. Besides, aren't the Brits underpaid, undersexed and under Eisenhower?"

"Harriet!" her father said scornfully. "I'll have no such talk coming out of your mouth, it's not lady-like."

Standing up, Harriet tugged at her blouse to straighten it. "Well, if you ask me, people seem to be too quick to cast aspersions on what they don't know and that includes you, Daddy. Have you even met an American soldier yet? I doubt very much that you have but when you do, I'm sure that you'll find them to be full of charm and good manners."

"And how would you know this?" he asked.

"I'm sure that Harriet must have meant that she's heard about their reputation on the wireless, didn't you, Harriet?" Stella asked her—raising her one eyebrow, as she waited for Harriet to comply.

Harriet, annoyed, sat back down in her chair. She nodded. "Yes, yes, that's right. I heard about them on the wireless."

Their father huffed. He left the kitchen and went upstairs to change out of his work clothes.

"So how do you really know what they're like?" Ruth asked Harriet.

Harriet leaned forward—closer to her sister. "One of the girls at the factory told me that she's been dating an American soldier for the past week. He seems harmless enough from what I can make out. He gave her gifts too. Chocolate and nylons."

"Nylons?" Stella asked. "Oh, what I wouldn't give for a decent pair of nylons."

Narrowing one eye—her forehead wrinkled, Ruth gave Stella a playful tap with her foot.

"Well, within reason I mean," Stella confirmed.

"So will you two be joining us for a drink in the pub?" Harriet asked.

Ruth relaxed her shoulders and then thought for a moment. "Well, if Stella needs a pair of nylons, who am I to stop her," she giggled.

•••

A Wartime Love
Shiralyn J. Lee

In the pub, Doris and Harriet were seated next to each other at the table. Stella and Ruth were on the opposite side. It was fairly quiet in the pub, just a couple of elderly gentlemen seated over by the wall, drinking their barley wine and the barman. They all looked disapprovingly at the girls for being there. One of the elderly gentleman shook his head—his stare cold, as he lifted his glass to his wrinkled mouth. But Harriet and Doris had the attitude of, 'if I'm good enough to work at a man's job, then I'm good enough to sit at the table he drinks from.'

"I don't like the way that man's looking at me," Harriet said as she felt the glare before she even caught sight of him.

Doris veered forward to look over Stella's shoulder. "He seems harmless enough. I'm sure that if the shoe was on the other foot, he would feel as uncomfortable as we are. Just ignore him and enjoy your drink."

The entrance door opened. A group of eight immaculately dressed American soldiers walked into the pub. Their broad smiles and perfectly white teeth were the first thing that the girls noticed.

"Oh, just look at those perfect teeth on that one, Harriet," Doris said, nudging Harriet's arm.

A Wartime Love
Shiralyn J. Lee

Harriet looked back over her shoulder—her eyes wide with intrigue. "Which one?"

Doris picked up her port and lemon and with her glass mid-air, she pointed her finger in his direction. Her line of eyesight also indicated to Harriet who she was keen on. "The second one on the left. Look at how perfect he is. What do you think, Stella?" she asked.

Stella swirled her port and lemon around in the glass and then took a sip. "Well don't ask me, I'm going to be a spinster, remember?"

Harriet tapped Ruth's hand. "Ruth, what about you?"

Before Ruth was able to answer, one of the soldiers walked over to their table. "Hello, ladies. Well, what a pretty sight it is to walk into a joint like this and find four attractive women all at one table," he said in his warm-friendly American accent.

Harriet's eyes darted—looking at both of her sisters and then at Ruth. She was smitten already.

Her tight-lipped smile and her one brow arched, Doris was the first one to respond to him. "Oh, it seems as though we have a charmer."

He slipped his hand inside his front trouser pocket and pulled out a packet of American cigarettes.

A Wartime Love
Shiralyn J. Lee

Flipping the carton open, he stuck one between his lips, where it hung from the side of his mouth, then offered the open packet around to the girls, who each in turn shook their heads and waved their hands to dismiss the offer. "Say, can I buy any of you ladies a drink?"

Gulping the remainder of her drink, Harriet slammed the empty glass down on the table. "I wouldn't mind one," she said with a cheeky grin on her face.

"Anyone else?" He looked at Stella, nodding suggestively. "You, perhaps?"

Stella waved both hands over her glass. "Oh, no. I'm perfectly fine with this one."

His buddies—at the bar, ordered their drinks and then two of them wandered over to the table. "Mind if we pull up a chair?" one of them asked. But before any of them were able to answer him, he had already turned a chair around from the table behind him, and with it facing backwards, he sat straddled over it with the back facing their table. He rested his arms on the chair back and in turn, smiled at each girl. "Well now, this sure is a pleasure."

Harriet, strongly infatuated, nudged Doris's arm. "It's a pleasure, he said." She looked down at her drink and giggled to herself.

A Wartime Love
Shiralyn J. Lee

"I'm Harry, this is John, Bruce, Doug, Gerry, Ralf, Richie and Frankie."

The girls—holding their glasses of port and lemon, smiled politely. It wouldn't do to be too forward with them, not while they were being watched, anyway.

The barman, standing behind the bar with a tea-towel in his hand, wiped glasses and placed them back on the shelf behind him. His unseemly glare didn't go unnoticed with the girls.

"I'm Harriet and these are two of my sisters, Doris and Stella. Joan is at home. And this is Ruth, Stella's friend."

"Nice to meet you, ladies," Harry said. The others followed with more smiles and nods.

Frankie was the one who was buying Harriet a drink. He pulled out a few notes from his jacket inside pocket and held the wad in his hand. There were disapproving looks and comments made by the elderly gentlemen, due to his rudeness in showing his money. This was a rule that none of the Americans understood. He paid for the drinks and even told the barman to take enough to pay for the next drinks for the elderly gentlemen.
Again, they shook their heads and whispered between themselves. He picked up the glasses and walked over

A Wartime Love
Shiralyn J. Lee

to the table. "There you go, sweetheart," he said to Harriet.

Harriet picked up her drink. "Oh, sweetheart. You're a bit presumptuous aren't you?"

"Well, isn't that what you Brits call each other?" Frankie jokingly asked her. He grabbed a chair and sat down next to her.

Harriet's face flushed with red. "Well, I still say you've got a nerve," she said with a half-smile.

Frankie slapped his thigh. "So, what music do you ladies like to listen to? That Vera Lynn dame's real popular, I hear."

Doris giggled. "Quite the charmer, aren't we."

Ruth and Stella had remained silent whilst the other two were being chatted up.

Bruce winked at Ruth. "And what about you, Ruth? Do you have a sweetheart hiding away somewhere?"

The colour drained from Ruth's face. Her lips pinched together, her head lowered, then turned away. She pushed her drink away from her, stood up sharply and plucked her jacket from the back of her chair. "I had best be going."

Bruce stood up. Confused, he stroked the chin of his chiselled face. "No, wait, don't go. Whatever it was that I said, I didn't mean to upset you."

Stella, unsure of Ruth's action, stood up and mirrored her. "I'll see you at home, sometime," she said to her sisters—kissing them each on their cheeks. As they both walked away from the table, they heard Doris whisper to the group of men that Ruth's husband was missing. For Ruth, it was a reminder that she was a wife—something that she hadn't been practicing of late, and for Stella, it was a reminder that her lover was a married woman and that neither one of them had brought his name up since she'd received the telegram.

Bruce sat back down in his chair and lit a cigarette. He watched the two women walk out of the pub. Exhaling the smoke and showing off, by blowing out smoke rings, he turned his attention to Doris. "So about your sister's friend. Does she always leave good company like that?"

Picking up her drink, Doris glanced over to the door—seeing her sister and Ruth walk out, she turned her attention back to Bruce. "No, no she doesn't," she said, her thoughts slightly muddled. "We've not known her for that long but she's been a hoot so far, considering what she's been going through."

A Wartime Love
Shiralyn J. Lee

•••

Walking out of the pub, Ruth, with Stella close on her heels, were met with greying cloud-filled skies. A light rain shower had just passed over. Droplets of rain seeped from the sagging leaves of sycamore trees. The fresh earthy sweet fragrance filled the air. Puddles had formed on the pavement and road.

Walking quickly, Ruth jadedly tried to catch her breath. "I'm sorry for walking out on your sisters like that." She tapped her forehead with the heel of her hand. "I feel so stupid."

Stella was unsure of why Ruth had reacted so hastily, nonetheless, she did understand that their predicament was a fragile one, and that what had happened between them, could well be the first and last time. She had no clue as to how to broach the subject.

Crossing the road, Ruth stopped her pace once she had stepped up on the pavement. She turned to face Stella. Her eyes turned darker, her voice taut. "This is not easy for me. He won't be the last person to ask about Clifford and I don't know what I'm supposed to do, or say. I'm married, no matter how we dress it up and even worse than that, he's missing. I can't act normal, not around people. I'm feeling something that I've never felt before. I'm feeling alive inside, yet I

A Wartime Love
Shiralyn J. Lee

suppress those feelings, because why should I be happy? Why should I be living a normal life, when Clifford is out there somewhere, possibly hurt, possibly calling out my name, because I am his wife. I've let him down and I feel that I'm letting you down and I'm so ashamed of myself for that." She raised her head to look both ways down the street. A young couple, arm-in-arm, walked along the other side of the street. The girl—her eyes filled with love, giggled when she stepped in a puddle. Her young beau pulled out his handkerchief from his coat pocket and wiped the tops of her now wet feet. Ruth re-focused on Stella. "I can't even stop right here in the middle of the street and hold your hand, or touch you in any way that would be considered affectionate. It sickens me that I have to live with a stigma, not only being married to a man and feeling that I have shamed our vows but also the fact that I am with you."

Stella licked her lips fast. "I'm scared. I'm scared that you'll reconsider what's happened between us and cast me aside for your husband, when and if he should ever return. That thought has my stomach in knots constantly.

There was an alley just ahead of them. Ruth suggested that they turn down it, as it was in darkness and out of sight. As soon as they were out of potential sight, Ruth took hold of Stella's hand. Raising it to her lips, she kissed the back of it. "I hurt inside," she whispered, her eyes dashing to the alley entrance ensuring no one would overhear her.

Stella bowed her head, resting it on Ruth's shoulder. She closed her eyes tight, her body rigid with frustration. "I feel dizzy and sick and my stomach is like it's filled with butterflies whenever I'm around you, and the hardest thing for me, is hiding all of this from my family. I have to listen to my sisters teasing me about being a spinster. I want to say something to them but I know I can't. Waking up beside you and then watching you as you still slept, made me wish that we could just be alone in this world together. I want everything to be peachy perfect."

Ruth glanced over her shoulder, again, checking the entrance of the alley, ensuring it was unoccupied. Sure that no one was in sight, she pressed Stella's back up against the red-brick-work of the alley wall, and then moved in close to her and engaged in a slow passionate kiss. She placed her hand beneath Stella's blouse, secretly caressing the small pert mound of flesh. Stella succumbed to Ruth's touch and placed her hands on the back of her head—kissing her hard and hungrily.

A tune being whistled by a man walking past the alley, quickly brought the two women to their senses.

They prised away from their kiss and stayed in the darkness of the shadows, watching him until he had walked away from them.

Ruth stepped back. She placed her hand on Stella's shoulder, keeping her at arms-length. She was nervous. She looked back-and-forth to the entrance and then to Stella. "We can never take this chance again, Stella. That was a warning for sure. What if he'd have caught us, what would have happened then? We must remain unseen, for both our sakes. There is no such thing as a peachy perfect world."

Stella hurriedly nodded in agreement. Just the sound of the man walking by had unnerved her. "Perhaps I was acting a little irrational just now but I am taking just as much of a risk as you are. I know that your reputation as a married woman is vital but I am a school teacher, if what we're doing is ever discovered, I know that I would be persecuted in just the same way that you would be."

Ruth lowered her shoulders and sighed heavily. Looking down at her feet, she touched Stella's forearm with the tips of her fingers—lightly moving them down to her hand. "Is it so wrong for me to be in love with you?" Lifting her head, so that Stella would catch the words as she bewitchingly whispered into her ear.

A Wartime Love
Shiralyn J. Lee

Stella felt as though her breath had just been taken away with the overwhelming element of surprise. "You...you love me?" Her mouth fell open, her eyes widened—her breath short.

Once again they were interrupted but this time it was female giggling. It turned out to be Doris and Harriet, who were giggling in between a conversation that they were having with Bruce and Frankie.

"So tell me, Frankie, why on earth would you call a tramp a bum?" Harriet asked him and then burst out laughing at her own words.

"And what's so wrong with calling a bum a bum?" Frankie asked her back.

Harriet and Doris laughed loudly.

Stella waited for them to be out of earshot. She ran her hand up Ruth's arm, grabbing her coat sleeve at the shoulder. "You said that you love me. Is that true?"

"More than I can ever explain," Ruth said in a soft confident tone. Even while they stood silent—patiently waiting for the group to pass, the pupils of her eyes enlarged—seducing Stella as she maintained her gaze in between the shadows and the dissolving daylight.

Stella's response was slightly delayed. She averted her stare, as she wanted to absorb the words that had been spoken to her. Her blinking increased drastically, as she plucked up the courage to reply. A timid cough paved the way for her words. "I love you too."

•••

Ruth held the bunch of keys in her hand. She picked out the front door key on the ring and as she went to place it in the lock, she dropped the set on the ground. Stella rolled her eyes and giggled. Ruth bent down and picked up the keys, then unlocked the door. She playfully pulled Stella inside and closed the door behind them. Stella walked backwards towards the foot of the stairs. A warm smile rushed over her face, her eyes glinted and her face lit up—she was contented. As her heel touched the bottom step, she raised out her hand to feel for the banister behind her. Finding it, she hooked her handbag over the end-post and placed her foot onto the first step.

Ruth gave a mischievous wink. Her eyes filled with vibrancy, her head slightly tilted to the side, she roguishly stepped toward Stella and before Stella could turn and run up the stairs, Ruth caught hold of her.

Stella squealed with excitement.

A slow coy smile travelled across Ruth's face, as she supported Stella by holding her around her waist, lowering her down onto the white-painted wood stairs.

A Wartime Love
Shiralyn J. Lee

Holding herself up by locking her other arm straight and gripping the step beneath Stella's head, she held her poise over Stella's body. Ruth's dark-eyes illuminated—exaggerated by her long black lashes. Her red-painted lips parted and she unashamedly moved in for a kiss.

Stella closed her eyes. The playfulness had fluently been replaced by passionate heavy-petting.

Raising Stella's skirt up over her legs, Ruth brushed her hand over the bare flesh, by using feather-like touches on her inner thighs. Stella flinched. She tilted her head back—her chin raised, her smile widened…her senses felt every inch of pleasure…

A Wartime Love
Shiralyn J. Lee

Chapter Eight

Stella called out the name of each child, as she ticked them off in the register book. She was thankful that they hadn't lost any more children recently, due to the fact that the bombings had decreased drastically over London. There were several empty chairs at this point—not one of those children had survived through the blitz. It was a constant reminder to Stella that these brave little mites had died a horrendous death.

Mr. Fletcher tapped on the glass pane on the classroom door and then summoned Stella to join him in the corridor.

"Children, continue writing. I shall just be out in the corridor," she told them. "Mathew, sit up straight, and Abbigail, please stop chatting to Andrew." She ambled over to the door and before she left the classroom, she pressed her finger to her mouth to show the children that she wanted silence whilst she was out of the room.

Mr. Fletcher seemed agitated. His jacket buttons were undone and his hands were clasped behind his back. His forehead furrowed, his eyebrows hooded over his eyes and his tightened lips turned down at the ends. "I've received a complaint about your behaviour towards another teacher in this school, Miss. Baxter, and I must say that I'm rather surprised, as well as disturbed by it."

"A complaint?" Stella was rather surprised herself, that was until she looked beyond Mr. Fletcher's shoulder and saw that Mrs. Davis with her eyes wide open, was glaring directly at them both.

Straightening his tie, he awkwardly stepped from one foot to another. "I'm sure that you are aware that Mrs. Davis has been a teacher at this school for quite a number of years."

"Yes, she did inform me of that, I hasten to say," Stella said firmly, then sucked her cheeks in and pouted her mouth.

Mr. Fletcher, who had been looking down at his shoes, as he attempted to shine them up on the backs of his trouser legs, looked up at Stella to see that she was staring in at Mrs. Davis's classroom. "Well then, I'm sure that you are also aware that she is a fine teacher and has never had cause to complain about another teacher before, Miss. Baxter?"

Stella kept her stare on the old woman, who remained at her desk staring back at her. "I do not

A Wartime Love
Shiralyn J. Lee

appreciate having to listen to her incessant screaming at the children in her class, when I am trying to teach just across the corridor. It's off putting for my own pupils and I'm sure for the other classes too. I know full-well that the other teachers feel the same as I do."

"Now, we all have to learn to get along, Miss. Baxter. I'm sure that we can resolve this issue and get back to what we are supposed to be doing here. Now then, let's just put this incident behind us and press on with our duties, shall we?"

This wasn't how Stella wanted this situation handled. Her eyebrows slanted inwards, with a wrinkle forming in between them, her mouth twisted to one side, a crease occurred in her cheek—she was annoyed, and Mrs. Davis had a clear view of that. "Are you through with me, Mr. Fletcher?"

"I have nothing further to add to the conversation, so I suppose that I am." His chin creased as he puckered his mouth. Placing his hands behind his back, he turned and walked away.

Stella returned to her classroom, acting in front of the children as if nothing had bothered her but inside, she was furious that Mr. Fletcher had only listened to one side of the story. Sitting at her desk, holding a pencil between her fingers, she tapped it relentlessly on the cover of a closed book that she was going to read to the children in the afternoon.

Her mood was soon distracted by a sound coming from outside, one that she couldn't determine. It was a new sound to her and even the children became preoccupied by it. The noise grew louder, it sounded almost like a spluttering motorbike but Stella knew that sound and somehow it didn't quite match. Mathew went to the window and peeled a corner of the blackout paper away from the glass pane. He drew in a sharp breath as his eyes witnessed something extraordinary. Then the noise stopped. In a matter of seconds there was a deafening explosion in the school playground. The frightened children screamed, some slid off their chairs and hid beneath their desks, others tried to run to the door and escape into the corridor. Mathew stood with his arms locked stiffly at his sides, his fists clenched tightly, causing his knuckles to whiten. His mouth gaped open, his eyes huge with fright, his scream—heart-wrenching.

Stella stood up fast. She knocked her chair over onto its back in the confusing panic. "Get down, everyone, get down," she squealed at them and then dropped down onto her knees. She peered out from behind her desk and called the children to crawl on their hands and knees over to her. The children were crying and snivelling but did as she had asked of them. Screams echoed from the other classrooms. No one had any idea that this was a V1 bomb launched directly from Germany.

The children huddled around Stella's desk. Air-raid sirens went off and then more sounds of spluttering bombs travelled over London.

"The cupboard!" Stella noted that the provisions cupboard near the classroom door would be a safer place for them to hide. She remained brave-faced and on her hands and knees, she told the children to follow her. When she approached the door, she reached up and turned the round-knob handle and opened it. She allowed the children to creep into the cupboard first. They sat down and huddled together, crying, cradling themselves and praying that this would all go away.

"Mathew, Miss. He's still by the window," Andrew told her.

"Oh god, no." Stella looked out of the doorway. She was petrified. She looked back at the frightened group of children. "You must stay brave. I'll only be a moment. Andrew, perhaps you could start a song and get the others to join in with you, could you do that for me?"

A Wartime Love
Shiralyn J. Lee

Andrew's eyes darted from Stella over to the children, who were whimpering and waiting for him to start a tune. He acknowledged the challenge with a quick nod and began to sing with the angelic voice of a choir boy.

Stella emerged from the cupboard. She had no time to crawl, so she ran as fast as she could through the room of disruption, with chairs overturned and desks moved from their original positions, until she reached Mathew. He had gone into shock and stood motionless, almost as if he had been frozen in time. She scooped him up into her arms and ran back to the small cupboard, joining the children, who were now singing like a choir group.

The spluttering noises and explosions were happening all around the school. They had to wait bravely in the darkness of the cupboard, until the raid was over.

Surprisingly, some of the children had fallen asleep, perhaps the fright that they had endured had taken its toll on their tiny little bodies. Stella gave them a gentle nudge to wake them. Tired, they moved.

"Is Mummy here, Miss?" Abigail, rubbing her eyes, asked Stella.

"I don't know, Abigail. We must go out and see if we can make our way home." She opened the cupboard door and peered out. She was faced with a horrific scene—one that she could never have imagined happening. There was nothing left of her classroom. Just absolute devastation. All that remained of the school was the cupboard that they were in and a portion of the corridor. Mrs. Davis's classroom was gone. The classroom behind Stella's was gone. She had no idea whether they had escaped and survived the bombings, or if they had been taken by complete surprise and killed. Not wanting the children to see how upset she was, she told them to all hold hands and walk in a line behind her. She held on tightly to Mathew's hand. He still hadn't spoken. "Stay brave, children," she told them. They all followed her in a single line—walking through drifting dust and over debris. "Cover your mouths with your free hands," she called.

Firemen and volunteers had fought hard to put out any fires that had been caused by the bombings. An ambulance was parked on the side of the road. Stella led the children over to the ambulance crew, where she informed them that she was a teacher at the school and had kept the children safe during the raid. A Red Cross van drove up behind them and the volunteers informed Stella that they would take care of the children. She went to let go of Mathew's hand but his clammy grip was tight.

She looked down at him to see that he was crying. "It'll be all right, Mathew. These nice people will take you to a safe place where your parents will be able to come and collect you from."

Mathew looked up at her. His chin quivered. His eyes still huge with fright. He trusted her…

The volunteer led the children away.

The dust began to settle and it was soon apparent that no one else had survived the blasts. Stella held her hand above her eyes to see the damage that was done to the school. Her legs turned weak and almost gave way when she was confronted with the actual damage. "Where…where…how…?" Panic ripped through her body. Stella felt lightheaded, her eyes rolled back…

•••

"Hey, Miss. Are you all right?" a man tapping her face asked her. Stella opened her eyes. She was sprawled out on the pavement and a strange man was looking over her.

"What…what happened?" she groaned.

A Wartime Love
Shiralyn J. Lee

The man, who was leant closely over her, sat back on his heels. "You fainted. I just caught you, before you hit your head on the ground."

Stella's eye flinched—she brushed her hand over it. The man reached out and took her by her arms, pulling her into a sit-up position. Her body ached, leaving her feeling weak, then her stomach turned over, making her want to vomit. She forcibly held it in. "The school...the children?"

"I'm sorry, Miss. There's nothing left of the school," he informed her.

Stella glanced over her shoulder, inspecting the aftermath. Her eyes stared...just stared, at the horrific absent space. She could feel her heart beating hard in her chest, too scared to breathe, yet her breath escaped from her mouth at uncontrollable intervals. She could not take her eyes away from the horror of destruction. Now she felt defeated. Nothing else mattered...nothing. Her body trembled—the colour drained from her face. Tears pooled in her eyes—a trickle escaped and rolled down her cheek, turning cold as it dripped onto the front of her blouse. She hugged her grazed shins and buried her face into her knees. Her self-worth had been put to the test—rendering her powerless.

•••

A Wartime Love
Shiralyn J. Lee

Opening the back door to her parents' house, shocked and confused, Stella didn't even remember the walk there. She was covered in dirt and dust. Black murky streaks crossed her face with a clear line running down each cheek where her tears had stained. She stood in the open doorway, her bloodshot eyes seemed frozen wide open.

Her mother and father were in the front room, they had just heard on the radio that the school had been hit during the raid and were frantic with worry. Doris and Joan had gone to the school, once the all clear sirens had sounded, to go to look for their sister. Harriet was with her volunteer unit.

Stella couldn't move. Her body was telling her that she was safe but her mind was playing tricks on her. Inside her head, explosions were going off, children were screaming—she was screaming…

Her mother rushed into the kitchen, with her father close behind her. "Stella, oh my darling, you're here!" she shrieked.

Stella, her trembling posture hunched, her palms clammy, her eyes wide—staring blankly into space, didn't respond.

"Oh, my, Stella, darling, you're home now," her mother then said softly, seeing that her daughter was not fully aware of her surroundings. She placed her hand on Stella's arm, however, Stella, still in the state of shock, jolted backwards.

Her father wiped his hand over his face, clearing the tears from his eyes. "She's in shock," he told her mother. "Come on now, Stella, you're safe now. Let us take you inside and get you cleaned up." He went to take her hand—again, Stella jolted back.

Stella, her mouth gaped open, tried to scream, no sound came out of her mouth. Her nostrils flared, her unblinking eyes bulged—still filled with frightful visions of death and destruction.

Joan and Doris ran down the alley, back to their house. They were screaming and crying, thinking that their sister had died at the school. They opened the back gate to see Stella, filthy and unmoving and their parents trying to talk her to going in to the house.

Joan reached out her hands to hug her sister—her mother whipped out her arm in front of, preventing her from connecting with her sister. "Stella, you're alive," she screamed.

Stella, hearing Joan's scream, jarred out of her shock. Her eyes slowly broke from their fixed stare, straying away from the open door, then locked on to her mother, who was standing next to her. "They're dead, they're all dead," she finally croaked.

Doris, who was still standing behind her, sadly nodded to her parents that her sister was correct.

"Stella, luv, let's get you inside and cleaned up. Would you like that, sweetheart?" her father asked her, as he looped his arm around hers and guided her into the house.

Her mother told her sisters to run the bath for their sister. They both barged ahead upstairs.

•••

The bath water had been filled to the five inch mark-line that had been drawn around the bottom of the tub—a government request that was part of the rationing for the war. Stella's mother carefully unbuttoned her blouse and slipped her arms out of the sleeves. Stella hunched her shoulders, shivering, as the cold air swept over her skin. Her mother then lifted Stella's arms up above her head and removed her silk full-slip, then her bra and matching cami-knickers. She held her hand, as Stella stepped into the tub and sat down in the warm water.

Her mother used a flannel to gently wash away the filth that had coated itself on her daughter's skin—

A Wartime Love
Shiralyn J. Lee

gently wiping it over her shoulders and down her back—rinsing it in the bath water and then washing her arms and legs. Joan sat on the edge of the bath and tenderly removed the hair-pins from Stella's hair, placing them on the sink next to the tap. She lathered up the soap in her hands and massaged it into her sister's hair, then used a jug to scoop up the bath water to rinse it out.

Stella's teeth chattered, as she grew cold from the chilling bathroom air.

"We thought that we'd surely lost you, Stella," Joan informed her, still rinsing her hair with the jug of water.

The water trickled down Stella's head, causing her hair to stick to her back. She shivered. "I kept them safe," she murmured. She sucked her lips in between her teeth, as she thought about what had occurred.

Her mother, who was on her knees, held the wet flannel in her hand—water dripped through her fingers and back into the bath. She sat back on her heels. "Your bravery saved all of those children, my angel. If you hadn't been so quick to think, they may have all been killed, and so may you have."

Stella, cradling her knees, her teeth chattering, turned to look at her mother. Her eyebrows, slanted upwards towards her furrowed forehead, her eyes, red and puffy from crying, her mouth, drooped downwards and her nose, red from the cold—she sighed heavily as she felt the emotional pain deep in her heart.

Joan reached for the bath towel that she'd placed folded, on top of the ottoman. She opened it up and held it out ready to wrap Stella in it. "There you go, sis," she said affectionately. She patted the towel over Stella's skin, trying to dry her faster. "Now then, let's get that hair of yours back to its glorious condition."

•••

Stella had dressed into her rayon flower-print pyjamas and black satin, with white rabbit fur-trimmed house slippers. She was in her bedroom sitting on her bed—her shoulders dropped and her hands placed over her face. The bedside lamp was on and gave off an oval glow on the large flower-print wallpaper behind it. Her chest heaving, Stella lifted her head and looked around the dimly lit room. She pressed her one hand over her stomach and the other over her mouth to suppress the sound and prevent anyone else in the house from hearing her deep sobs.

Her family were downstairs, whispering amongst themselves, so that she couldn't hear what was being said.

A Wartime Love
Shiralyn J. Lee

The front door opened and closed loudly. Stella jolted and whimpered at the sound of the slam. It was Harriet and she had brought Ruth home with her. They rushed into the front room, where they found everyone apart from Stella, discussing what had happened.

Ruth, her eyes large and glassy, glanced around the room. "Where...where is she?"

Stella's mother, seated in her armchair, gave a brittle smile. "She's upstairs in her room, resting, I hope. She will be quite happy to see you, Ruth."

Ruth averted her eyes downwards—her head lowered, as she shamefully thought about their secret love for each other. She was desperate to see for herself that her lover was safe and well. "May I go up and see her?" she asked Stella's mother.

"Of course you can, dear, but if she's still sleeping, it might be wise to leave her be."

Harriet, who was in front of Ruth, headed for the door. Ruth edged closer to her and graciously planted her hand on her arm, stopping her in her tracks. Harriet—her nose scrunched and her upper lip arched, didn't understand why her sister's friend had stopped her.

A Wartime Love
Shiralyn J. Lee

"Please, could I go and speak with her alone? I really don't mean to be any bother to anyone, I just…" A long sigh escaped her. "I'm sorry, please forgive my bad manners, you go ahead of me. That was totally selfish of me to expect you to wait."

Harriet's eyes narrowed. "Surely we can go together?"

Ruth rolled her shoulders back and stood tall. "Yes, of course we can."

•••

Ruth followed Harriet into the hallway. Just as they got to the foot of the stairs, the phone rang. Harriet picked up the receiver of the black Bakelite phone. "Hello. Ah, Aunt Millicent. It's Harriet, how are you?"

Ruth stood at the foot of the stairs, her hands gripped over the end-post of the banister, as she waited for Harriet to deal with the phone call. She turned to look at herself in the antique hall mirror that was hanging just by the front door. She stared at her own reflection. The shadows cast over her face made her look tired and much older than her age. Perhaps the constant air of worry and stress over not knowing her husband's whereabouts and how things would evolve between her and Stella, had taken its toll on her looks. She pinched her cheekbones and patted down a few flyaway strands of hair.

"Okay, Aunt Millicent, I'll just fetch Daddy now." Harriet put the receiver down on the half-moon shaped shelf and stuck her head into the open doorway of the front room. "It's for you, Daddy. It's Aunt Millicent. She sounds terribly quiet." She swung around and then led the way upstairs. Almost every step creaked, as the two ventured up together.

Stella was seated on the edge of her bed when they entered. Ruth brushed past Harriet at the doorway and lunged into the bedroom. She dropped to her knees at Stella's feet. "Oh my poor darling," she said breathy. She placed her head into Stella's lap—her eyes closed and her thoughts only for the woman whom she thought she might have lost in the bombing. Her lack of eye contact with Harriet had betrayed her, as Harriet was now even more suspicious of the relationship that she had with her sister.

Stella, her shoulders hunched and her head hung low, gently patted Ruth's hair with both of her hands. She breathed heavily as she felt the relief of holding her beloved Ruth close to her.

"Stella, what's going on here?" Harriet asked her. Her head cocked to one side, her forehead filled with lines, her mouth twisted up to one side.

Stella looked up at her sister. Her eyes fogged with tears, she gave off a pleading look. "I can't tell you," she whimpered.

Ruth clasped her hands into Stella's and turned her face to look up at her lover from her lap. "I couldn't bear it, I couldn't bear the thought of losing you," she cried softly. Her tears ran from her eyes and dampened Stella's pyjama bottoms.

Harriet, her mouth gaped open, her eyes huge and glaring at the pair, took a step back. "Stella?" She looked behind her at the open doorway.

"Please, Harriet. I beg of you not to say a word to anyone, especially Mummy and Daddy. They just wouldn't understand what we have."

Harriet took another step back towards the doorway. "I don't know what it is that you have but this isn't natural."

A shrill came from downstairs. It was their mother.

Harriet, hesitant at first, left the room and ran down the stairs to find out what had just occurred.

Stella drew in a sharp breath. Ruth stood up. The pair immediately responded and headed down the stairs.

"What is it, Mummy?" Stella asked, finding her mother collapsed in her armchair with her hands slapped over her face, patting her cheeks. Joan and Doris were seated on the settee. Both had deadpan expressions on their faces.

Her father was leaning over the fireplace, his head pressed against the wall. "It's your cousin James. Aunt Millicent just informed us that he's been killed over in Germany. Damn this blasted war!"

"Cousin James is dead?" Harriet asked. She sat down next to her sisters on the settee. Her issue with Stella's predicament had been pushed aside for the time being. "I can't believe it. He was such a nice and kind boy." The colour drained from her face and she slammed her eyes shut so tightly, that wrinkles appeared at the sides.

Ruth stood closely behind Stella. She placed her hand gently over her shoulder, seen as an act of compassion by Stella's parents and sisters. Stella could feel her warm breath on the back of her neck—it was comforting for her.

Harriet opened her eyes—her stare toward Stella and Ruth was unyielding. She curled her lips with icy contempt—her nostrils flared and her face turned crimson with annoyance. "I'm sure that Ruth would rather be in her own home and not here seeing all of our sorrowful faces?"

Ruth—her head lowered, glanced sideways at Harriet. She felt her sarcasm, even though no one else had picked up on it. "I will only go if Stella asks me to leave," she said gently.

Stella looked back over her shoulder. She reassuringly patted Ruth's hand. "No, don't go. I really want you to stay."

Harriet glanced away from her sister. Tears developed in her eyes and rolled down her flushed cheeks. "I have so many fond memories of Cousin James," she said sadly.

The war had finally touched them with the sorrow of death.

A Wartime Love
Shiralyn J. Lee

Chapter Nine

Harriet laid in her bed—her hand tucked beneath her pillow, she lay in a foetal position. Her gaze was to the curtain. With the windows blacked out, the street no longer offered her the dim light that she once had from the lamppost outside. She raised her head and in the darkness of the room, she looked over at Stella's bed. It was hard for her to make out but the silhouette of Stella and Ruth tucked up in that small bed of hers, gave Harriet cause for concern.

"Psst, Stella, are you awake?" she whispered.

Stella laid on her side with Ruth, wearing a pair of her pyjamas, behind her—her arm relaxed over Stella's arm. Stella opened her eyes. "What is it?" she whispered back.

"I want to know what's going on between you two."

"Harriet, will you please go to sleep. I can't talk about it now." Stella whispered back sternly.

•••

An hour later, Harriet sat up in her bed. She turned her bedside lamp on and stared over at the other occupied bed. She was uncomfortable with her thoughts about her sister's secrets.

Stella awoke. She was confused as to why her sister was glaring at her whilst she had been sleeping. "What's the matter, Harriet?" she asked her, still half-asleep.

Harriet lowered her head but looked up with her child-like eyes. "You're supposed to be my closest friend, as well as my sister but I've hardly seen you over the past few months. You spend all of your time with Ruth." She heaved herself forward on her bed— her face buried into the bedspread to prevent anyone from hearing her cry.

Stella pushed back the sheets and climbed out of her bed. She sat beside her sister on her bed and placed her hand on Harriet's back, stroking her sympathetically— her watchful eyes on the door in case anyone was to overhear her. "Ruth is more than a friend to me, dearest Harriet."

Ruth stirred, as she heard the disturbing conversation across the room. She got out of bed and closed the bedroom door to prevent the others from waking and hearing what was being discussed. She sat on the other side of Harriet, hugging herself, as she had felt the chill in the room. "There are things that we cannot explain, Harriet. Things that happen between two people that were not planned. I can see that you are distressed, so I will not add to your uncertainty anymore. I have a special relationship with your sister."

Stella gave a sharp glare to Ruth. She shook her head in an effort to prevent her from saying anything else incriminating.

Harriet stopped sobbing and lifted herself up from the bedspread, sitting in between her sister and Ruth—her eyes red and swollen, her chin quivering. "Special?" She looked back and forth at the pair.

Stella nervously sat up straight. She licked her lips, followed by rubbing the underside of her nose. "I think what Ruth was trying to say, is that we are really good friends—"

Harriet planted her hand on Stella's leg. "Please don't lie to me, Stella. I know that there's more to your friendship than you say there is. I know, because I can see with my own eyes. I see how you look at each other, how you touch each other. I see how Ruth holds you when you are sleeping in the same bed." Harriet's eyes were huge with antagonism. "You still treat me as a child."

A Wartime Love
Shiralyn J. Lee

Stella shamefully bowed her head, looking at her hands that were tugging apprehensively at the bedspread. "I love her, Harriet."

Ruth expelled her breath with relief—her gaze dipped momentarily as she absorbed the monumental words being spoken so freely by her lover. A red glow applied itself to her cheeks as her eyes rose to meet the gaze of Stella's, their vibrancy lit up her face.

Harriet snivelled, her eyes darting between her sister and Ruth. "I've done something that I'm so ashamed of." She covered her eyes with her hand to hide her look of shame. "You weren't around and I was angry and because he paid attention to me, I just didn't care."

Stella leaned in close and grabbed Harriet's arm. "What do you mean, you did something you're ashamed of?"

Harriet slowly prised her hand away from her face. Her eyelids half-covered her eyes as she looked down at Stella's lap. "After you two left the pub, we drank our drinks and then Frankie and Bruce said that they wanted to go and see a movie. We went to the picture house but spent more time kissing than we did watching the stupid bum-holing movie. He said the right words, Stella. Words that I needed to hear. He even gave me a chocolate bar."

"Harriet, what are you trying to say?" Stella asked her.

"We left the picture house. Doris stayed with Bruce and finished watching the movie. I told her that Frankie was going to walk me home, as I had a headache. I lied to her. Instead, we walked to the park and when we came across a patch of bushes and trees, we went and laid down amongst the thick foliage. Stella, I let him touch me there. Oh god, I'm so ashamed of myself."

Stella's face reddened with anger. "You mean, what I think you mean? Harriet, think really hard about your answer. Did you remove your knickers and let him do it with you?"

Harriet shamefully nodded and then let out a cry. Stella placed her hand to the back of her head and snuggled her into her chest area. She cradled her and told her that everything was going to be all right.

"I told him that I'd done it before and that it was no big deal. He thinks I'm a whore now, doesn't he?" she sniffled, feeling dejected.

"No he doesn't, Harriet." Ruth assured her. "I'm sure that he is an honourable man, after all, he is an American and helping us to fight this dreaded war. That says a lot for him, doesn't it?"

Harriet raised her sodden face. "I suppose you're right," she whimpered.

"My poor precious, Harriet," Stella said. She kissed her on the top of her head and stroked her hair affectionately. "The war really has changed us all, hasn't it?"

•••

It was Christmas Eve. Stella and her sisters had made paper chains and hung them up on the ceiling, around the walls and over mirrors and pictures hanging on the wall. A small pine tree in a pot of dirt had been decorated with more paper chains and placed on the sideboard, where everyone was able to see it in the front room. It gave little in the way of joy but at least it was able to offer some sort of normality in the way of celebrating the traditional holiday. Sprigs of holly had been painted with a concoction of Epsom salts and water that acted like glitter and had been placed on top of the fire-place mantel. Because farmers had opted to grow crops in favour of livestock, there had been a shortage of livestock produced, so with no turkeys available, the Minister of Food suggested an alternative option. Sausage meat was to be moulded and formed into a turkey shape and parsnips used as their legs. It was then wrapped in strips of bacon and roasted in the oven. Sprouts, squash and carrots accompanied the meal. Pudding was plum duff with custard, a variation of spotted dick.

Doris had been dating Bruce and had invited him and Frankie over for Christmas dinner. Stella had invited Ruth. They sat around the table that their father had set up in the front room. The fire was lit. It crackled and spat, as the orange glow flickered over the coals. Tall candles in a three armed candelabra, dressed the centre of the table. Their father sat at one end and their mother at the other end, everyone else sat on either side of the table. Doris had been unaware of Harriet's predicament with Frankie and didn't know that they had been intimate. Harriet was quiet. She blushed with embarrassment every time that Frankie's name was mentioned in the conversations that were going on around the table.

"This is mighty swell of you folks to allow us into your home like this," Bruce said to Mr. Baxter.

"We don't like to see anyone left out on such a special occasion. It wouldn't seem right," he replied, as he tucked into his plum duff pudding.

"You sure can cook, Mrs. Baxter," Frankie complimented her.

A Wartime Love
Shiralyn J. Lee

"Well, I've had years of practice," she answered, feeling appreciated. "Your mother must be so proud of you with those good manners of yours."

"I'm kind of proud of her too," he said, scooping up a spoonful of custard and quietly slurping it into his mouth. "Say, Harriet, you haven't been around much these past few weeks. I hope you'll give me another chance to take you out again."

Stella gritted her teeth. She had perceived his intentions as other than honourable by his suggestive date. "Harriet's been rather busy, being as she's an ARP. She's been working overtime and I'm sure that you understand the importance of women in the workforce over here right now."

"Well I sure as heck do. In fact, we American soldiers are hearing great things about how you women are handling things just fine over here, while most of your men are over in Germany, killing Germans.

"So, Frankie, whereabouts in America are you from?" Mrs. Baxter asked him.

Frankie politely placed his spoon into his bowl and wiped his mouth with the napkin that he had tucked into his shirt collar. "Well I happen to come from a small town in South Carolina, a place called Orangeburg but my folks moved to Brooklyn when I was twelve. I can honestly say that I've had the best of both worlds and now I've experienced the British way of life too."

"I bet you have," Stella muttered.

"And I'm from Savanah, Georgia," Bruce informed them.

"Well it seems that there's a lot of Burgs in America, don't you think?" Harriet rudely joked.

Frankie rested his elbows on the edge of the table and propped his chin up with his hands. "Perhaps there is but you seem to have a lot of mouths over here, so I'd say that we are pretty equal in the lack of originality for naming towns, don't you say?"

Mrs. Baxter frowned at her daughter. "Harriet, I don't think that was called for. Rudeness is not how we have brought you up, any of you." She looked at her daughters, one by one, ensuring that they understood her request.

Bruce picked up his rucksack that was at his feet. He opened it up and pulled out some gifts that were wrapped in brown paper and tied with string. "We thought it only fair to exchange gifts with you folks, being as you made us feel welcome in your home, an' all." He handed them out, firstly to Doris, then to Mrs.

Baxter, then to Mr. Baxter, then Joan, then Harriet, then Stella, then Ruth.

They all unwrapped their gifts. American chocolate brought smiles to their faces. Although before the war, chocolate was in great supply in Britain but since the war, it had been a rarity. These were extremely well received gifts in the Baxter household.

Joan had been quiet throughout the celebratory meal. Her thoughts had been preoccupied with her fiancé and how she hadn't received any letters from him for a while. She had picked at her food like a bird and not really cared for joining in the celebrations. She looked around the room to see everyone was enjoying themselves, except for her. "Daddy, would you mind if I had another glass of Port?"

Her father raised his brow. "And why would a daughter of mine suddenly want a second helping of Port?"

Joan bravely stopped herself from tearing up. "Because I miss Will, Daddy, and I haven't heard from him and I'm worried. What if something awful has happened to him, I couldn't bear it?"

Her mother gave a sympathetic gaze towards her. "Well, I for one wish we could have met him before he left. I'm sure that he's fine, sweetheart. We must remember that perhaps writing letters isn't the foremost important thing on his mind at the moment."

"I know, Mummy. I know it's quite selfish of me to even think that he should write to me but I can't help what my mind and heart are feeling."

Her father picked up the bottle of Port and poured her a half-glass. "There, you deserve that. Now, I suggest that we make a toast to the king."

"To the King and absent friends," they all toasted together. Straight after, they all stood up and sang the anthem, 'God Save Our Gracious King.'

Mr. Baxter reached over to the cupboard behind him and picked up his pipe and Tabaco. He opened the packet, pinched some Tabaco and stuffed it into the bowl of his pipe. He stuck the mouthpiece between his lips, lit a match and sucked a few times until a puff of smoke evolved. Bruce and Frankie lit up their own cigarettes—the three of them soon filled the room with the smell of smoke.

"Well, we have mince pies to finish off the day with," Mrs. Baxter told everyone. She stood up and collected the pudding bowls from around the table, then headed out into the kitchen.

Frankie leaned to his side to whisper to Harriet. "Say, I'm getting the feeling that you don't like me anymore."

"You got what you wanted, Frankie. It's not going to happen again," Harriet, covering her mouth with her hand, informed him.

"Say, I think you're a swell kind of gal."

"You got what you wanted from me, Frankie. I'm not the kind of girl that you think I am." She stood up quickly, her stance stiff and erect, her little fists clenched at her sides. "I'll help you with the mince pies, Mummy." She moodily waltzed out of the room.

Frankie was surprised by her sudden need to leave the room. He inhaled on his cigarette and looked thoughtful—his elbow on the table, he watched the door, waiting for Harriet to walk back in. He could hear her talking with her mother.

Bruce interrupted his absent mind, by encouraging him to join in the conversation he was having with Doris, Stella and Ruth. "I said that we have a couple of buddies who would just love to take these swell looking ladies out on a date."

Frankie turned to face his hosts. "Yeah, sure. They were the guys who were with us at the pub," he told them.

Stella, her face expressionless, glimpsed at Ruth from the corner of her eye. "I'm sure that we can make do without any men in our lives for the time being," she told them with a high-moral tone.

Mr. Baxter sat back in his chair and smoked his pipe. "So have you been on many missions over Germany?"

Frankie drummed his fingers on the edge of the table. "Now that would be telling tales, Mr. Baxter. I think that we should just say for now, that we've taken part in flying over Germany and we've taken down a few of their menacing aircraft."

Harriet walked back into the room holding a white china plate of mince pies and her mother brought a pot of tea on a tray with matching cups and saucers—they tinkered with her movement. "Well, at least we get to use the best china," she said. "Tea anyone?"

"I must say that I'm becoming quite partial to your tea drinking habit, Mrs. Baxter," Bruce told her. He picked a mince pie from the plate and bit half of it away. "I've heard all about these and now I've finally tasted one."

A Wartime Love
Shiralyn J. Lee

Stella and Ruth had secretly given themselves the job of watching Frankie and making sure that Harriet was not put in any kind of compromising position, if he were to say the wrong thing.

They all drank tea and swapped stories, comparing growing up in England and America.

It grew dark outside and it was time for the two Americans to leave the Baxter house. They gave thanks for the hospitality and Bruce said his goodbye to Doris in the privacy of the front garden, behind a bush. She giggled. Frankie had asked Harriet to accompany him to the front door, so that he could speak with her.

Standing on the doorstep, with his one hands in his front pocket and holding a cigarette in the other, Frankie stood relaxed. "Say, I kind of find that you've gone off me."

Harriet leant against the door frame. She fidgeted with her bracelet. "I'm never making that kind of mistake again, Frankie. I did something so awful and I'm so ashamed of myself." She raised her eyes level with his gaze. "I've never really been with anyone else before you. I lied. I lied because I wanted you to like me."

A Wartime Love
Shiralyn J. Lee

Frankie threw the butt of his cigarette down on the path and stepped on it. "Jeez, Harriet. If I'd have known, I would never have…well, you know."

"Well you did and now all you think I am, is a whore," she said, keeping her voice low.

"Quite the opposite, Doll. I like you. You've got spunk. And who could resist looking into those adorable innocent eyes. I like you like I've never liked any other gal before."

The pupils of Harriet's eyes dilated. "Really?"

"Honest to god, Doll." He crossed his fingers over his chest. "Now may I see you again and may I say that my intentions will be as an honourable gentleman."

Harriet stood up straight. "Perhaps I might agree to see you again but there'll be no funny business."

"Swell. I'll be seeing you real soon, Harriet Baxter. So can I steal a quick kiss before I go?"

Harriet leaned forward and gave him a peck on his cheek.

"Well, I suppose that will have to do for now." He walked away whistling—his hands tucked inside his pockets. "Come on, Bruce."

•••

A Wartime Love
Shiralyn J. Lee

Boxing Day was back to normal, as far as warfare was concerned. It was a cold misty eerie kind of day. A crow squawked in a tree just outside of the Baxter house and in the distance, the sound of a single motorbike echoed through the streets.

Everyone in the Baxter household was awake and had eaten their breakfast. They were in the front room. Joan had taken up knitting with her mother, Doris sat on the middle seat of the settee, reading a romantic Victorian novel. Harriet sat on a footstool in front of Joan, with the yarn of wool wrapped around her open hands and her mother carefully taking it and wrapping it into a ball. Stella sat on the end arm of the settee and Ruth sat on the end seat next to her. They both looked fairly innocent, as far as their family were concerned, all except for Harriet, who had completely forgiven them for their secrecy, as she too had one that they were both aware of.

Their attention was slowly drawn to the oncoming sound of the motorbike outside in their street. Its spluttering noise grew louder—their eyes grew wider. No one spoke. Mrs. Baxter got up from her seat and went to the front door to see whose house the rider was going to. They had many neighbours with husbands and sons fighting in Germany and knew most of them personally. It was a heart wrenching sight to see anyone get a knock on their door by one of these riders.

The motorbike stopped in the street outside of their house. Mrs. Baxter watched the young man as he got off it and then searched his pockets for the telegram that he was about to deliver. He looked at the door number on the house next to the Baxter's and for a short moment, Mrs. Baxter thought that he was going to go to Mrs. Green's house. Her son and husband were both fighting for their country. But the young man did not go toward her house. Instead, he gradually looked at Mrs. Baxter, who was standing on her own doorstep. She was confused as to why he was approaching her front gate.

She looked to the houses on her left and then to her right. "Who are you looking for?" she asked him, still certain that he had chosen the wrong house.

He continued his walk towards her. Clenching his jaw, he maintained his silence. The telegram was in his hand, ready for her to take. "I'm so sorry to be delivering this telegram to you," he said quietly, his eyes looking to the ground.

Mrs. Brown took the telegram from him and looked at the name that it was addressed to. A frown crossed her forehead, her mouth drooped downwards. She found it difficult to catch her next breath. The young man with his head lowered, turned around and walked away.

Silence still filled the front room, as the others waited for word of who had received the telegram. As their mother walked slowly back into the front room—her eyes down, Joan gave out a whimper when she saw the envelope in her mother's hand. She trembled with fear. This telegram could only have meant one thing. Her Will was either missing, or dead. Her mother, with one hand over her mouth, handed it over to her. Joan—her hand shaking violently, reluctantly took it from her hand. She opened it up—all eyes were on her. Her father got up from his chair and stood at her side—his hand placed gently on her shoulder. She read out the words that had been typed on the paper. "We are sorry to have to inform you that Mr. William Dunn, was killed whilst on duty, fighting for his King and country."

Joan gripped her stomach as the pain of realisation at losing her fiancé hit her hard. There was nothing that could have prepared her for this news. Her woeful cry was one that would stay with everyone forever. Her father—a man who rarely showed his emotions publicly, had tears streaming from his eyes as he closed them and lowered his head.

A Wartime Love
Shiralyn J. Lee

"They send the telegram to their next of kin," Joan cried out. "I was that person, because Will had no one, he only had me, and now he's gone. I'll never see him again. They took my Will away from me, Mummy."

"Oh my poor, Joan," her mother cried for her. She held out her arms for her daughter to be wrapped in.

Joan knocked her knitting from her lap onto the floor and stood up—her mother's embrace was the only thing protecting her from the hurt. "I want to die, I want to die and be with Will," she cried into her mother's chest.

All that her mother could do was cradle her. Everyone felt hopeless.

A Wartime Love
Shiralyn J. Lee

Chapter Ten

They say that time is a great healer but for Joan, every day of the wretched war was a constant reminder of her loss. She, along with countless other mothers, fathers, wives, fiancés, sisters and brothers, would wake every morning with bitterness towards the people around them, towards their nation and towards the war.

•••

Harriet and Doris were careful enough not to mention that they were seeing Bruce and Frankie, and Stella would spend most of her time at Ruth's house, to avoid causing any suspicions about their relationship.

The war—the threat of being bombed—the continuation of raids carried on, and yet, still the nation did not break. Churchill made his broadcast speeches on the wireless, people listened and agreed, or disagreed with his decisions. Destroyed buildings were cleared, more allotments were created where those buildings had once stood, and farmers were instructed by the government to increase their productivity.

A Wartime Love
Shiralyn J. Lee

• • •

Orangey-yellow candle flames flickered, as the wax dripped down the sides of the white tapered sticks. Tiny shadows danced over the small flower-patterned wallpaper. Ruth's cold fingertips graced themselves down Stella's swan-like back, as the pair lay beneath the bedspread, huddled together—naked and fresh from having just made love. Their hearts still beat fast, their smiles—not ready to leave their faces. Their noses cold from the cool room temperature, their faces—flushed. Their emotions delicate and fragile, their gazes innocent and enticing, and yet, behind those adoring eyes, images of the sensual acts that had just taken place.

Ruth positioned her lips on Stella's shoulder, where she kissed her tenderly. She brushed her hair away from her neck and nibbled on the edge of her earlobe. Stella—her eyes bright and filled with love, giggled. Her preoccupied emotions had been aroused.

With a simple tone, Ruth whispered into her ear, "I love you."

A warm smile enhanced Stella's pleasured mood. "I love you too."

Their eyes locked in a desirable gaze—Stella—her fingertips touching the silky-smooth skin of Ruth's thigh, as they laid in silence, feeling the euphoric rapture.

•••

Sliding her hand along Stella's arm, Ruth slipped out of her side of the bed. The wooden floorboards were cold to the touch. They squeaked as she walked barefooted around the bed and over to the chair in the corner of the bedroom. She picked up her camiknickers and in front of the cream-fringed vanity lamp—her bent-over silhouette, elegantly gave off a pictorial image, as she stepped into them and slid them up her legs.

Stella propped herself up on her side, her head rested in the open palm of her hand—her attentive eyes engaged in the picturesque appearance of her lover. "You are beautiful, even when I can't see you clearly."

Ruth straightened up. Her head turned to face Stella. Even though her figure had been cast by shadowed lighting, it was still apparent that she had a radiant smile across her face. "You are a romantic, aren't you," she said—the tone of her voice playful.

Their romantic mood was short lived, when the sounds of planes in the distance could be heard. Stella shot out of bed and grabbed her blouse and skirt from the floor. There was no time for escape. They ran downstairs, both frantically dressing in the clothing they had in their hands. But as they reached the hallway, a British Spitfire flew right over the house. The sound was distinctive, not like a German plane that tended to have a splatter sound to its engine. Then there were squeals and cheers outside in the street. Ruth opened the front door to see many people standing in their front gardens and looking up into the air, turning around as they followed the plane in its path.

"That's right, give it to the bloody Jerrys!" an elderly man griped, as he stood at his front gate shaking his fist in the air.

The Spitfire was in a dogfight against a German Foke-Wulf—flying over the houses and then up into the skies and disappearing behind the clouds. The Spitfire shot at the German plane, the German plane machine gunned at the Spitfire but the Spitfire won the battle and sent the Foke-Wulf to its destiny—shot down in flames into the sea.

The incident created a buzz on local radio broadcasts—with the news broadcasters reporting that it would be the main topic of conversation for days to come, and that it would restore the very hope and faith that had been declining with the British people in recent months.

A Wartime Love
Shiralyn J. Lee

∴

It was late afternoon. Outside, the winds had whipped up. Cloud formations motioned across the sky, leafless trees swayed and anyone caught walking, wrapped themselves in warm coats, gloves, scarfs and hats.

Ruth and Stella had made themselves a cup of tea and were in the front room lounging on the settee. Stella, seated on the end cushion, stroked Ruth's hair as she laid with her feet up and her head rested on Stella's lap. They spoke of their favourite books and poems, and of the foods that they missed because of the rationing. It felt good for them to reminisce, as it gave them both fond memories of what they once used to have. Their mood was that of tranquil and contentment.

"I'm going to have to get a job at the factory," Stella told her.

"Are you sure? Surely there must be a school somewhere for you to teach?"

Stella lowered her eyes to look down at Ruth. A slight smile emerged but it was not one that represented happiness. "I don't think that I could ever indulge in that again. I grew fond of the children, I know that I shouldn't have but I'm a big softie. I couldn't go through the hurt again if anything was to happen."

A Wartime Love
Shiralyn J. Lee

Ruth raised her hand to Stella's face—her forefinger pointed. She stroked Stella's nose playfully. "Well then, perhaps I should get a job at the factory too."

A loud knock on the front door interrupted their intimate conversation. Ruth lifted her head up from Stella's lap.

The knock came again, only this time it was louder. "Stella? Are you in there?" Harriet yelled. She pushed her fingers through the letter box to open it and shouted. "Stella, it's me, Harriet, let me in, please."

Ruth sat up quickly and Stella rose from her seat and sprung to the front door. She opened it fast to see Harriet—her eyes filled with tortured emotions, her face red from the chilled wind. She found it hard to catch her breath and without delay, she flung her arms around her sister and sobbed.

Stella was surprised. She had no idea what had caused her sister to be so broken. "Harriet, what's wrong? Please tell me, sweet darling, Harriet."

Harriet turned her head from Stella's shoulder to face her. She was so child-like and innocent. "Please take me inside."

•••

A Wartime Love
Shiralyn J. Lee

Ruth had made Harriet a cup of tea and placed a biscuit on the saucer for her. She planted it down on the table next to the chair that Harriet was seated in. "Please, take off your coat and stay a while."

Harriet's mouth turned down at the sides, her eyelids were low, her nostrils flared. "I don't know what to do," she managed to blab.

"Do about what?" Stella asked her, seeming confused by her whole being there.

Harriet slapped her hands over her face. Her breathing became erratic. "Stella, I'm pregnant. I'm having Frankie's baby."

Stella's mouth fell open in disbelief. She sat on the arm of Harriet's chair and placed her hand on her shoulder. Her sigh was deep and lengthy. "Have you told Mummy and Daddy?"

Harriet moved her hands away from her face and sniffed hard. "You're the first person I've told. I didn't know what to do. Oh, Stella, I only did it the once, I've been so stupid." The tears continued to develop in her eyes and flowed down her cheeks, spotting into her lap.

"And what has Frankie said about all of this?" Ruth asked her sympathetically.

A Wartime Love
Shiralyn J. Lee

"He doesn't know. I only came to realise it myself this morning. I've missed my monthly, it should have been three weeks ago and it still hasn't happened."

Stella could feel her sister tremble uncontrollably, as she soothed her hand over her back with a gentle touch. "You must tell him, Harriet, and if he's a proper gentleman, then he will do the right thing and marry you."

"Marry me? He's fighting a war for our country, risking his life to help ours and I'm to expect him to marry me?"

Ruth sat up straight on the settee and clasped her hands in her lap. "He had a part in getting you pregnant, Harriet. And I'm sure that he would not be so callous to allow you to go through this without doing the honourable thing, so you must tell him."

Harriet nervously tugged at her skirt. "I've been so foolish…" Her eyebrows furrowed, she lowered her head—her eyes closing slowly, as she felt the power of shame engulf her.

Stella, her eyes on Ruth, shook her head. "No, you haven't, Harriet, darling."

•••

A Wartime Love
Shiralyn J. Lee

Later that day, the high-winds turned into an afternoon of bleak rain and thick darkened clouds that had engulfed most of the south region. Stella had had decided to take a very scared Harriet home.

Harriet chewed on her nails, as they turned into Rodney Street. She was scared of what her parents were going to say, and that anyone she knew, would shun her for being an unmarried pregnant woman. "I can't face them, Stella. I don't know if I can ever face them about this."

Stella knew that this was going to be a difficult task in hand. Harriet was the baby of the family, the innocent one, the one who they should have all looked out for. In a strange way, she felt as though the guilt should lay upon her. Perhaps if she'd have been more attentive to her sister's loneliness, maybe she wouldn't have found herself in this predicament. She looped her arm into Harriet's and tapped her fingers from out of her mouth. "I'm not saying that this is going to be easy but there will be a time soon that you will be showing signs of being with child. It would be wise to prepare everyone concerned beforehand. You'll be all right, you'll see."

Stella opened the front gate and let Harriet walk through first. The creaking hinges had alerted their mother that someone was approaching. She opened the front door and greeted her daughters with a beaming smile. "Well I wondered where you had disappeared to, Harriet."

Harriet, her shoulders slumped, her hands in her coat pockets, lowered her eyes and gave a half-smile.

"Hello, Mummy," Stella said, walking by, touching her cheek and giving her a kiss.

Her mother watched Stella, as she walked into the house. "Stella, sweetheart. You're looking awfully thin, is everything all right? Perhaps I should fill you up with a bit of tinned rice pudding. Would you like that, dear?"

Stella looked back over her shoulder. A smile crossed her face. "Oh, of course I would, Mummy. Perhaps a dollop of jam with it as well?"

Harriet barged straight through to the kitchen without saying a word.

"Is everything okay with your sister, dear?" her mother asked Stella.

Stella came to a stop at the kitchen door. She turned—her face expressionless. "I think that you and Daddy had better sit down for this. There's something that you need to know."

A Wartime Love
Shiralyn J. Lee

Her mother shut the front door. "I don't like the sounds of this at all, Stella, dear," she grumbled.

•••

One of the hardest things for a young woman to tell her parents, was that she was pregnant and unwed. There was no exception for Harriet either. After informing them about her condition, her father, speechless, walked out into the hallway, picked up his coat and cap from the wooden stand by the front door, and left the house without saying a dickey-bird. Her mother had remained in her armchair patting her chest—a habit that she had whenever there was something to do with a disturbing nature. Her face pale, her eyelids heavily hooded over her sad eyes, she rose to her feet and headed off upstairs to the bathroom.

Stella, unnerved by the lack of shouting, or upset being displayed, followed her mother to see if she was all right.

She found her holding a dish containing small pieces of old soap. She picked up a flannel and placed the bits of soap into it and then twisted the flannel tightly. She dipped it into a little warm water in the sink, then twisted the flannel harder, squeezing the excess water out. She opened the flannel to reveal a newly formed piece of soap. A smile presented itself across her face.

A Wartime Love
Shiralyn J. Lee

"There, now we have a new bar of soap. I can't stand it when it gets to that yucky end bit."

Stella lightly placed her hand on her mother's wrist. "Mummy, are you all right?"

Her mother sighed deeply. Her whole presence was a mess. Beneath the apparent smile, she appeared broken. She put the soap down on the side of the sink, ready for use. "There are mothers out there, in this street even, in this city too, who have lost their sons and daughters in horrific circumstances. They'll never have their child to hold, or be able to tell them that they love them ever again. Yet, an unmarried pregnant girl is the news that brings shame to a family. Why is it that we spurn those who we should be protecting?"

Stella rested her head on her mother's shoulder. "I don't know, Mummy."

Joan, who had been sleeping in her be, had been woken by the conversation. Half-asleep, she wandered out from her bedroom. Her eyes red and puffy, her face gaunt, she leant against the bathroom door rubbing her eyes. "Who's pregnant?"

"Hello, Joan. It's good to see you finally up and out of bed," Stella said, after not seeing her sister for a while, knowing that she had taken to her bed with depression after Will's death.

Joan raised her hand and wiped her eyes. Her voice trembled as she searched for her words. "Every day that I wake, I feel repulsed that my Will died and he never got to meet any of you."

Stella lifted her head from her mother's shoulder. She held her hand out for Joan to take. Joan placed her hand in Stella's. A pained smile exchanged between them.

Stella's mother, still clutching the flannel, wiped the soap scum from the edge of the sink with it. "Harriet," she said, choosing not to look at Joan.

Joan didn't instantly absorb what her mother had just said to her. "What about Harriet?"

Her mother stopped scrubbing the sink. Her chin quivered. "Harriet's pregnant."

Joan's eyes widened to their fullest. She drew in a sharp breath and smacked her hand over her mouth, shaking her head in disbelief.

•••

Stella had left the house to go and look for her father. She had an idea where he had disappeared to and headed off to where there had been newly founded allotments. She found him crouched down in the soil, digging with his bare hands. His eyes were red and swollen, his cheeks flushed from the chilled air. Harriet had always been his little girl and Stella could tell that he was hurting badly.

She stood at the edge of the allotment—her hands in her coat pockets, her scarf wrapped around her neck and tucked into the collar of her coat. The tips of her shoes just touching the freshly turned over soil. "I feel partly to blame, Daddy. I should have been looking out for her."

Her father stopped digging. He looked up at her—he was angered. "That man was in my house and sat at my table, eating my food. Food that we can barely afford to feed ourselves, let alone give away to complete strangers.

Stella's face was red from the cold. Her tears welled in her eyes but she dare not let them fall. "I'm so sorry, Daddy."

He clenched his fist and pounded his knee. "Sorry isn't going to fix it. Sorry won't take back what he did to my little girl. There's been nothing but disarray, first with the war, then with Joan's fella and now this. I don't even know how your mother's going to cope with all of this and that bloody bastard had better do the right thing and marry her, before anyone suspects that she's…she's…" He closed his eyes shut tight. He

A Wartime Love
Shiralyn J. Lee

couldn't even bring himself to say that his daughter was pregnant.

    Stella yanked her hands from her pockets and clasped them tightly behind her back—her cheeks sucked in and her mouth pouted, she held her head low. She knew that she could never tell him, or anyone, about her secret affair with Ruth.

A Wartime Love
Shiralyn J. Lee

Chapter Eleven

The wedding plans were a hurried affair, causing whispers amongst the extended members outside of the Baxter family. There was no organised fancy ceremony—no beautiful white-gown for Harriet to boast her striking looks in. Instead, she wore her favourite crepe dress and a hat that Doris had given her. She also held a small posy of flowers, mainly filled with ferns, as flowers were in short supply and what she did have, were handpicked from their back garden. She was able to wear a pair of nylons that Frankie had given her as a gift a few weeks previous and a handbag that matched her shoes. The only glamorous thing about her that day was her hair. She had fashioned it high on top of her head in a waved roll, giving it the elegance and glam of a movie star. Frankie proudly wore his military uniform and so did his entourage of American soldier buddies.

Bruce had brought along his box-camera and took a photograph of the happy couple standing outside by a leafless oak tree. They were shivering from the cold—everyone was but they didn't let it stop them from at least enjoying a short-lived formality. Frankie and his crew were only given a few hours leave to celebrate his matrimonial day.

Stella, Doris, Joan and Ruth had been Harriet's bridesmaids and all wore their Sunday best clothes, none of them matched in their attire.

Mr. and Mrs. Baxter had taken a back seat in all of this. They went to see Harriet marry, however, they were not too inclined to show their support. To them, this was a shot gun wedding and no doubt soon enough, tongues would be wagging about the whole sordid affair.

There was sadness in Harriet's eyes. She knew that she had disappointed her family—that they would be disgraced, once people knew of her condition. Frankie had even spoken of them living in America once the war was over. It was an option that she was seriously considering—her family were not aware of this suggestion, as of yet.

Frankie was all smiles. His buddies were encouraging him with remarks of, 'Now you have two bosses to answer to,' and, 'Well there goes another drinking buddy.'

Harriet's father on the other hand, wasn't too impressed by the lack of respect for his daughter. He spent most of his time shaking his head with disapproval—seeing the American's as a loud and bad-mannered race.

Frankie gave Harriet a kiss on her cheek, while at the same time he fumbled in his jacket pocket for his packet of cigarettes and lighter. He flipped open the top of the packet and drew one out, sticking it between his teeth, he snapped open the lighter. A puff of smoke rose into the air, as he exhaled, then he plucked it from his mouth and held it between his two fingers. "Hey, Bruce, take a photo of me kissing my new bride, I want to be able to look at her when I'm up there, flying around."

Bruce stood in front of them and took a photograph. "There you go, Buddy. That ought to be a nice keepsake."

Harriet blushed.

Frankie looked over at Harriet's sisters and parents. "Say, we need to have one with all the family too." He summoned Harriet's family to stand next to them and have their picture taken together. Stella, Ruth, Joan and Doris immediately stood alongside Harriet. Their parents were more reluctant. "Mr. and Mrs. Baxter, come on. Let's all have a family picture taken, what do you say?" He tossed his cigarette to the ground and stepped on it and then winked at his new in-laws.

Feeling the pressure, they walked over and joined the group to have their picture taken. Everyone smiled, apart from them.

"You look absolutely radiant, Harriet," Stella whispered to her just after the photo was taken.

Harriet broke a delicate smile. "Thank you."

Frankie had been aware of Harriet's parents being none too thrilled over their whole wedding fiasco. "I'll take good care of your daughter Mr. Baxter," he said confidently. "And I'm sure that when we've settled down in Orangeburg, once the war is over, you folks are more than welcome to come visit us at any time. My mother sure would love to meet you all."

Stella frowned at Harriet. "Orangeburg?" she cried out.

Harriet's sisters gathered around her like clucking hens protecting an egg, all speaking at the same time. Harriet felt bombarded. She took a step back—her hands waving out in front of her to stop them from fussing any further. "Stop! Just stop, please. This is my wedding day and so far all I've had, is my parents disapproving scowls and completely ignoring Frankie.

A Wartime Love
Shiralyn J. Lee

And now this! Have you all forgotten that I'm carrying Frankie's baby? Do you not think that for me to leave all of you behind and set up a life in a country that is completely strange to me and with Frankie's family, people that I've never met, is going to be easy for me? I haven't even agreed to go yet."

Stella, Joan and Doris, feeling guilty, stopped their outburst.

"I can't tell you what to do, Harriet, but I will say that I'd hate it immensely if you did leave," Stella told her. Doris and Joan nodded their heads in agreement. "Surely, Frankie, you can see how much this is going to hurt us all?"

Frankie, confused by the commotion, scratched his head. "Well, from what I see, you British seem to have a strange way of treating your unmarried pregnant ladies. Sure, it wasn't planned but I love your daughter," he said to Harriet's parents. "And your sister," he said to the three angry looking women standing at Harriet's side. "I want what's best for her. Can you give her that?"

Mr. Baxter looked down at his feet. He too felt shamed. He took off his hat and held it over his chest. "Harriet, can you ever forgive me for spurning you? I'm so sorry, my angel."

Tears rolled down Harriet's face. "Oh, Daddy." She flung her arms around him. "I don't want to go anywhere. I just didn't want to bring any more shame to you."

"I'm not ashamed of you, Sweetheart. I just needed time, that's all."

Frankie, his hands on his hips, his smile showing his white teeth, turned to his buddies. "Well it seems as though we might just be staying after all."

As they stood around the newlyweds, a squadron of Spitfires flew overhead. Everyone looked up at the fighter planes and cheered…

Harriet threw her arms around Frankie's neck. She kissed his face. "Thank you, Frankie. Thank you for not making me leave my family."

"Ah, anything for you, Doll."

•••

Furniture shops and garages had been transformed into factories, to allow more fighter planes to be built. The demand was high and every single woman between the ages of twenty-to-thirty were expected to do their part in the war effort and work.

A Wartime Love
Shiralyn J. Lee

Stella and Ruth had gotten themselves a job at the same factory as Doris, being as Doris had put in a good word with the floor manager.

It was Monday morning and their first shift had started. Doris walked them over to the manager's office. "I'm going to leave you here. You'll be fine, I have to go and start my work, someone will be with you shortly. Don't be nervous, Stella, you look frightfully concerned." She walked away, leaving the pair outside the office.

A tall thin woman stepped out of the office—her hair tucked under a turban. "You must be Ruth and Stella? Doris has been talking all about you two. I'm Mary Benson. Now then, first things first. You'll not do with what you're both wearing. Tight clothes are essential for working in a safe environment. I'll grab you some overalls and you can change over there." She pointed to an area at the side of the office, where they could change in private. There was a metal cabinet behind her that housed folded overalls. She picked one each for Ruth and Stella. "Also, you'll need to cover your hair. We wear turbans for two reasons, one, for keeping your hair from getting tangled in the machinery, and two, you can have your hair in rollers and have a nice hair-do for the evening." She handed them the overalls and turbans and waited while they changed.

"Well, how do I look?" Ruth, turning around with her arms out, joked with Stella.

Stella held her hand to her mouth and giggled.

They walked out, ready to be shown their first task.

"Now, there are just a few simple rules that you do need to follow for safety reasons. Your nails must be trimmed. Long nails can cause an injury. No high-heel shoes. Wide, low heels will do just fine. You must wear safety goggles on certain jobs and report any skin irritations, or injuries immediately. If you are sitting down for long periods of time, you must sit up straight, to avoid backache, and I will advise you that you'll need your full eight hours of sleep, and a good diet, to keep you energetic. No slice of toast for lunch, that won't fill you up. You have a place in the war effort, absence affects all other workers. Taking an extra day off can, and will, affect production. You must do your part for your country. You will be paid £1.25 a week. There, I think that I've covered the most important rules for now." She walked them past a group of women, who were wearing goggles and eye shields and were already hard at work. Sparks were flying as they soldered pieces of metal together.

"What will we be doing?" Stella asked Mary.

"I'm going to put you both on riveting. Sylvia and Elsie will show you both the ropes."

Sylvia, a dark-haired woman, with a few greying strands, in her late-thirties and from a working class background, wiped her nose on her overall sleeve and then sniffed hard. Her eyes narrowed, she looked Stella up and down. "The blonde one can sit over there and this one," She pointed to Ruth, "can work next to Elsie."

Stella held her hand out. "I'm Stella and this is Ruth."

Elsie, a mousy type of looking woman, looked up. She smiled. "Hello, I'm Elsie as you gathered."

Sylvia ignored Stella's hand gesture. "That's enough chit chat. Let's get you ladies started," she ordered. She sat Stella at her work station and Elsie showed Ruth to hers.

They both put on their protective goggles.

They were given a few instructions on how to use a rivet gun on the cockpit shells and then left to their own devices, to get on with the job in hand. Sylvia checked on Stella's work every now and again, to make sure that she was following the instructions that she had been given.

"So, what were you doing before?" Elsie asked them both.

Ruth stopped working. She smiled at Elsie. "Oh, I wasn't working at all. My…"

"Not working? What, the likes of you too good for work, are they?" Sylvia interrupted her.

"She's married to a man in the military. He's overseas and has been reported as missing," Stella told her firmly. "Have a little compassion, at least."

Sylvia reeled her head back. "What, you gotta stick up for her, have you?"

Ruth glanced sideways at Stella. She shook her head discretely, to let her know that she didn't want her telling Sylvia anymore about her personal life. Stella, embarrassed, looked down and carried on with her work.

Sylvia gave a short sneering smile. "And what about you, blondie? What did you do, or do you think that you're too good for the workforce as well?"

Maintaining her calmness, Stella spoke elegantly. "I was a school teacher, if you must know."

"Oh, and were you too good for this kind of work before the war?" Sylvia mocked, looking at Elsie with a winning grin.

"No. If you must know, the school that I taught at was destroyed during an air-raid. I managed to save the children in my class but unfortunately the rest of the school stood no chance, they all died."

"Oh, now I know where I've seen you before. My sister's little boy, Mathew, he's in your class. Or rather, he was," Elsie said to her. "You saved all of them little kiddies, didn't you? You're a hero, do you know that?"

"I did what I had to do," Stella answered coyly. She hated the reminder of that day.

"Well, you may be a hero to the kiddies and their grateful parents but in here, you're just like one of us. No time for snobbery of any kind, do you hear? You work and you get paid," Sylvia said sharply.

Ruth pursed her lips and squinted her eyes—she glared directly at Sylvia. "We're here to do our bit for the war, we're not here to be ridiculed and insulted by the likes of you, or anyone else."

Sylvia laughed loudly. It was a sarcastic type of laugh. "Says she who hasn't done a day's work in her life. See that poster on the wall over there? Well that's a picture of Rosie the Riveter, she's a real woman, a hard working woman. Perhaps you should take note of that."

"Okay, Sylvia, I think you've made your point to the new ladies," Elsie said with an advising tone to her voice.

Sylvia rubbed her nose with her leather glove. "I'm just letting 'em know how it is around here, Elsie, that's all."

Ruth lowered her head and muttered, "I think we got it."

Sylvia's hard eyes darted from Stella to Ruth, narrowing, as she focused on the delicate female attempting to use the rivet gun for the first time. "There's no place for anyone who can't do this job. Better make sure you get it right the first time. There's lives at risk if you don't."

Elsie leaned toward Ruth. "Don't mind her. Her bark is much worse than her bite. She just doesn't trust too many people." She then turned her quiet voice into a whisper. "And she is one for liking the ladies, so she probably likes you really."

Chapter Twelve

The war continued on, raids over England were unrelenting. Medieval buildings had been ruined, schools demolished, homes obliterated and the death rate climbed.

Ruth and Stella had been working at the factory for a few months. They were now part of the Royal Air Force Auxiliary. Women were trained to fly the finished planes and flew them to the RAF bases, where they were then turned over to the flight crews and armed ready for battle.

Harriet was now in her sixth month of pregnancy. She still lived at home with her family whilst Frankie stayed at the barracks with his crew.

Doris had found herself a nice English Officer to date. She had decided not to continue her relationship with Bruce after the realisation that she could end up leaving her family and move to America to settle down with him. She was not born into a family who took these decisions lightly. Her new beau was a gentleman to the extreme and had turned her head. There were even talks of marriage on the horizon, once the war was over.

Joan had recuperated from Will's death. She got herself a job as an ARP and was very strict with curfews and banging on doors and calling lights out to the occupants inside their homes.

•••

It had been a fairly hot day, so Ruth had opened the top small window in the front room and the kitchen window, to allow the air to flow through. Stella had put an Anne Shelton record on the gramophone. She held her hand out for Ruth to take and the two—hugging each other, moved slowly to the music. They were entranced with the sultry mood—one that was leading up to an intimate moment. But this mood was interjected by knuckles rapping hard on the front door.

Ruth reluctantly prised herself away from Stella's hold. "I'll get rid of whoever it is." She kissed Stella lightly on her cheek and then went to the front door. She opened the door—her eyes widened to their fullest, when she saw her husband Clifford standing on the door step, smiling, as he surprised her by being there. "Clifford," she whimpered.

A man with dark-hair, brown eyes and smiling, held out his hands. "Hello, luv. Well, are you going to let me in?" he asked moving towards her for a welcome home kiss.

Stunned, Ruth reeled back. "Yes, yes," she said politely, opening the door wider for him to enter.

He stepped inside the doorway and as he passed her, he awkwardly kissed her on her cheek. There was an ungainly smile between them both, as though they had become strangers in their absence.

"I'll go through to the front room, shall I?" he asked heading for the front room.

Ruth closed the front door. As he disappeared in to the front room, she sighed heavily. Now her life was going to be even more challenging for her.

"Hello. Who might you be?" he asked Stella, who was on her knees looking through a pile of Ruth's vinyl records.

Stella looked up at him and smiled but her smile soon broke, as she recognised that he was the man in the wedding picture on the mantel. "Clifford?"

"Well, that's who I am. Now I'm at a loss as to who you are."

Ruth, unsure of how to act, entered the front room. She was nervous. "Clifford, this is Stella. She's been a really good friend to me." Her dark eyes were filled with fear. She was concerned for Stella's feelings and for their secret affair. "Clifford, I received a telegram that you were missing. I had no idea that you were even alive." Her hands trembled—she held them behind her back.

Stella got up from the floor and held her hand out to shake Clifford's hand. If Clifford knew how to read a person's eyes, he would have known that Stella was agonizing inside over his being there. Not recognising her pain, he shook her hand.

"Well, it's nice to know that Ruth has been with a friend and not on her own during all of this time. I know it's been hard for everyone."

Stella gazed at Ruth. The pleading in her eyes was eminent. "Perhaps I should leave and allow you two to talk."

"No!" Ruth rebutted immediately.

"So, are you not going to ask me where I've been?" Clifford asked his wife.

Ruth's eyes locked on to Stella's "Please stay, Stella." She ignored the man who had returned from wherever he had been.

Stella lowered her gaze. She knew Ruth was failing at keeping their relationship a secret. "So please tell us, Clifford, where you have been?" she asked, ashamed that he had been ignored by his wife in favour of her.

Clifford sat down on the settee. He patted the cushion next to him for his wife to join him. Ruth looked at Stella in a way that was asking what to do. She reluctantly sat down next to him, remaining stiff and awkward, as he patted the top of her thigh. Ruth brushed his hand away.

"Our team were caught in a crossfire situation between the Americans and the Germans. It was a bloody situation. American aircraft were flying over us and gunning at the Germans. The Germans were firing back at the Americans with tank fire. We were a team of ten men and had to hold back and hide. Then American ground troops arrived and we joined them. The battle went on for hours. There was so much death on both sides. I heard American men scream out for their mothers, as they laid injured and dying in the field. The smell of blood was overwhelming, I never knew it could have a smell like that. I saw men's bodies blown to pieces, faces blown off." His leg was restless and shook—he held it still with his hand. "John Maxwell, one of the men on my team, he was crouched down behind a rock, hiding from the Germans, as they marched forward in our direction. We were all scared. God, I thought we were all going to die. He held his rifle up and leaned his face against it. Gunfire was coming at us from all directions. A bullet hit his rifle and sent shrapnel flying. He died instantly but most of us, who were hiding out, were hit with pieces of the shrapnel. I got it in my left shoulder and arm. The next thing that I remember, is that I'm in an American field hospital. I woke up and had no idea who I was."

"So you lost your memory?" Stella asked him.

"Yes. I was eventually taken to a hospital in France. I didn't understand a bloody word that any of the nurses said. It took months for my memory to fully return."

"And now you're back here," Ruth said with a short tone.

Clifford looked at her wryly. "I've been through things that no man should have to."

"We've not exactly had too much of a great time here, either," Ruth told him.

"Ruth, there's something that I need to tell you. I'm not sure if I should say it with your friend here."

Stella awkwardly walked over to the doorway. "I'll leave. I think that would be best for us all."

A Wartime Love
Shiralyn J. Lee

"No!" Ruth snapped at her. "I don't want you to leave." She looked at Clifford coldly. "I know that I must be coming across extremely callous in all of this but, Clifford, you have been gone for a long time. I know you've put your life on the line and I understand that you thought you could come back here and we would pick up where we left off but…"

"Hold on," Clifford interrupted her. "I'm not here to come home. I've been given my orders to get back out there and fight again. This war isn't going away anytime soon. I wanted to come here to make sure that you were all right and that I had something to tell you and I wanted to do it properly. This war can make us do things that we would consider unthinkable. I never thought that I could do this. I won't be coming home again…"

Ruth's forehead wrinkled with her frowned look. "What do you mean?" she asked him.

Clifford sighed. "You'll be fine, Ruth. I'm sure that you'll meet the right man eventually. I just don't think that I'm the one. We married in a hurry. It was an impulsive decision and I think we both know that. We did it just because I was being sent out to fight in this damn war nonetheless, we did it for all the wrong reasons but the one reason we should have married for, wasn't there. I didn't love you, Ruth, luv, not in the way that I should have."

Ruth drew in a sharp intake of breath. Her fingers twitched, as she clasped her hands together on her lap. "What are you saying, Clifford?"

"I've met someone. Someone I really want to be with. Madeleine Sablon. She's a nurse, a French nurse and she taught me to remember again. Only when I did, I realised that there was something important that I needed to do and that was to let you go."

Stella stepped back into the centre of the room. "You mean you're asking Ruth for a divorce?"

Clifford gave a tense smile. "Yes I am."

For a few moments, silence was the loudest thing that filled the room.

Ruth shifted sideways on the settee to face Clifford. "I'm so sorry that I was so rude to you. You surprised me and I thought you had died, I honestly did. There's no excuse for my rude behaviour, please forgive me."

His expression lightened. "I already did, Ruth," he said.

"You say her name is Madeleine? Is she in love with you too?"

"Yes. We plan on being together after the war is over. I didn't want you to find out from someone else that I'd met her. There are a few soldiers who like to brag, you know how it is."

It was like a huge relief had been lifted from Ruth's shoulders. She hadn't counted on Clifford's return and she definitely hadn't considered that he may have met someone else in spite of the war. "Perhaps I should get you something to eat. We have plenty of bread for us all."

"No, I'm fine. I have to be back at the barracks in an hour. I just wanted to say goodbye." He stood up and moved over to the doorway. "It was nice meeting you, Stella." He took one last look around the room. "I don't think there's anything that belongs to me here. If there is, just give it to a charity shop. I won't be needing it where I'm going."

Ruth got up from the settee. She brushed past Stella, their eyes met in disbelief. "Let me walk you to the door, Clifford," she said.

Clifford opened the door and stepped outside. He turned around and smiled at her. "Please take care of yourself. I know that I'm leaving you during a desperate time for our country, however, I don't think that I could have gone back into Germany with this weighing heavily on me."

Ruth gripped the side of the door, her face pressed up against it. "Clifford, we've all seen and done things that are out of the norm because of this war. None of us are innocent."

Clifford nodded his head in agreement. His departure was awkward as he walked down the path and opened the gate. He shut the gate and gave another smile at Ruth, who stood leaning against the open doorway. She stared at him, watching until he had disappeared down the street.

Stella put another vinyl record on the gramophone and called Ruth into the front room. Ruth closed the front door and joined her. They could hardly believe what had just happened.

The song played—the sound scratchy, as the vinyl turned with the needle tracking its way through the record groove. Stella held out her arms to embrace Ruth once again. Holding her gently, she placed her cheek on Ruth's shoulder. "I love you," she said, with a hushed voice.

Ruth closed her eyes—her hands around Stella's waist. "I love you too."

A Wartime Love
Shiralyn J. Lee

●●●

The war continued on. It was considered the deadliest conflict in history and ended with the enemy surrender in 1945. England had paid with hefty losses in lives and in communities. Lone German bombers would fly overland and target anything that had meaning. A train at a station in Cirencester was attacked by a Luftwaffe bomber plane. As far as the people of the City were concerned, it was a needless attack. Coventry, a beautiful City filled with medieval buildings—attacked in an air-raid. Loss of life was so severe that the funerals were held as one mass service and the bodies laid to rest in one long grave. Major ports and towns around the country suffered much devastation and death but life still managed to find a way to flourish.

A Wartime Love
Shiralyn J. Lee

A Wartime Love
Shiralyn J. Lee

Fifty Years Later

Ruth and Stella were now in their late-seventies. They have been happily living together over the decades. As far as they were concerned, they would tell people that they were two old spinsters, just living together for the company but there were a few people who knew about their secret love. Even Sylvia had become an ally, once they had put their bickering aside.

Harriet gave birth to three children, two girls and a boy. Jane, Violet and John. She and Frankie are now grandparents and still very much in love.

Doris ended up marrying her Officer beau. They have two children together and three grandchildren.

Joan never married. Instead, she found solace in helping those who had lost members of their families during the war. She never fully recovered over losing Will.

Their parents died within close proximity of each other, in the early-fifties. The house was sold and the proceeds split between the four girls.

Clifford and Ruth divorced once the war was over. He married his Madeleine and lived the rest of his life in Nice, France, until his death in the late-eighties. Ruth wasn't sure of the exact date because she was told a few years later by an old acquaintance, who had fought with him in the war.

Stella and Ruth had remained living in their home in Duncan Terrace. They'd spent their entire life together—inseparable. There hadn't been a day go by where they didn't say that they love each other. Love was very important to them. It was war that had brought them together and they wanted to remind themselves that it was love that made them stay…

~The End~

A Wartime Love
Shiralyn J. Lee

Coming Soon

A Wartime Romance: A story based on World War 1

Other Published Books

A Victorian Romance
The Dark Cully's Mistress
The Submissive Scullery Maid
Ruby Tipped Globes
Captain Caiterina O'Creagh
Captain Caiterina O'Creagh and Elizabeth Bromley
The Memoirs of Ivie Smith
Stop in the Name of Love
Vampire Changeling
Loving the Pink Kiss
Pink Crush
Pink Seduction
Lesbian in Question
Chasing Yesterday
Tell Me What To Do
Paige Bleu Series
She's on the Ball
Touching Gloves
Erotic Spirits
Sex, Ropes and Chains, Safe Word Series…BDSM

A Wartime Love
Shiralyn J. Lee

A Wartime Love
Shiralyn J. Lee

About the Author

Growing up in England, I spent most of my youth in Kidderminster before moving down to sunny Devon. In 2006 I moved overseas to Canada where I now happily reside with my wife Janice.

I have many books published, all written under the lesbian genre. I love to write in different time eras, ranging from early 1800's through to modern day. I have also made each story line unique with their plotlines by using situations from my own personal experiences. Some of my work is romantic with light sensual sex scenes, and some are featured with stronger explicit sex scenes and coarse language to intensify the drama. I prefer to give my readers a wider selection of choice; we are all different in what we like to read.

Printed in Great Britain
by Amazon